MW01701456

BLURB

Flutes of Paradise is a novella of experimental nature and perhaps a tapestry or collage of sorts. Follow Leopold to the end of existence in an uproarious world of intrigue, alien, and dreamshape, where the only way to love is to love complete, ask questions, and tell stories with eyes wide open.

PRAISE

Flutes of Paradise ripsails along with the most absurd lucidity imaginable. Surprising. Important. Fantasy-Real. Like the superfly-wicked Cruzbike Q45.

— PETE O'BRIEN

FLUTES OF PARADISE

PETE O'BRIEN

Xyloquirk Books

Published by Xyloquirk Books, www.xyloquirk.com. *Flutes of Paradise*. Second Edition. Copyright © 2025 by Pete O'Brien. All Rights Reserved. Ebook ISBN: 978-1-951390-41-9. Print ISBN: 978-1-951390-40-2. Previously published as *Visions* (First Edition) by Pete O'Brien (*Visions*. Copyright © 2025 by Pete O'Brien).

The following chapters in *Flutes of Paradise* were originally published as short short stories on the Xyloquirk Books blog (www.xyloquirk.com) in 2023: Cured, Zoom Birds, In the Warehouse, Shock Sun, After Dark, The Homecoming, The Orbific, and Let Me Explain. The Danger Exit appeared on said blog in 2025. The illustrations for said shorts were adapted from the full color illustrations on the blog.

Visions has been fully revised, and is published with the updated title of *Flutes of Paradise* for the Second Edition. Cover Art and Design by Pete O'Brien. Text Illustrations, Art, and Photography by Pete O'Brien.

Flutes of Paradise is a work of fiction. The characters and events in the story are imagined things. Figments. Any resemblance to actual people and events is coincidental. In a case that there is a reference to something in reality, the doodad is used fictitiously.

No part of this book may be reproduced in any form or by any electronic or mechanical means, including information storage and retrieval systems, without written permission from the author, except for the use of brief quotations in a book review.

DEDICATION

To the one who is somewhere
if it turns out not to be with . . .

And to those who imagine with gusto and succumb not to the screens of diminishment.

And to various extraordinary canines.

EPIGRAPH

Hey. I'm ready for the journey now.

—ANONYMOUS

CONTENTS

1. Essential 1
2. The Danger Exit 3
3. Encore 10
4. Magical Ring 12
5. Cured 14
6. Zoom Birds 18
7. In The Warehouse 23
8. Shock Sun 27
9. After Dark 29
10. The Homecoming 34
11. The Orbific 39
12. Let Me Explain 43
13. Something Has to Happen 49
14. The Astronauts - The 59
15. Entirely Nondescript - The 61
16. Wanderer - The 62
17. Delirium - The 64
18. Clues - The 65
19. Into the Night - The 67
20. Interview - The 70

Chapter 21 76

Chapter 22 77

Chapter 23 78

Chapter 24 79

25. Once Upon A Sweeping 80

Chapter 26 81

Chapter 27 82

28. Elemental 83

Chapter 29 85

Chapter 30 87

31. Judge 89

32. Mellow Jacket 92
Chapter 33 94
34. Orange Juice 95
35. Rosary at Noon 96
36. Cow Charmer 97
37. Shockwave 99
Chapter 38 103
39. Turquoise 104
40. Torn 105
41. Her Face 107
42. Mistakes 109
Chapter 43 111
44. Then A Princess 112
45. Gallery 116
46. Apple 118
47. Knowledge 119
48. Collars 120
49. Fire Escape 122
50. The Way 123
51. Soulreach 125
52. Camera 126
Chapter 53 127
54. Cloud Storm 128
55. War 129
56. Amplified 131
57. The Fine Point 132
58. Solid Cherry? 134
59. Understood in Time 135
60. Humbongo 136
61. Zinc 137
62. Raspberry 138
63. Wanderer 139
64. Journey 140
65. Homespun 141
66. Relevancy 143
67. Painter 144

68. Pale Stone 146
69. Animation 148
70. Dictator 149
Chapter 71 150
72. Cancer 151
73. X 152
74. A Natural Prism 153
75. Library 154
76. Rows Upon Rows 155
77. At the Start 156
78. Fugacious 157
Chapter 79 158
80. Steam: The Common Good 160
81. Hair 161
82. Sweat 163
83. Speck 164

Afterword 166
Also by Pete O'Brien 168
About the Author 169

FLUTES OF PARADISE

*

❧ I ❧

ESSENTIAL

In my dream, the hands of a little girl slip away from her at birth. A great cloud of azure pajamas allows it, and everyone is so busy staring up at the sky in their hideous stockings, grabbing for the flannel, that they forget, some things you can't control. But you can fight. And you can fight to the death.

It's like this. When the elders come home, with their heads in shopping bags by their sides, searching for their cerebellums in ancient telephone books (yet another artifact of time), there are tears in my eyes as I remember their younger selves grilling hamburgers and hot dogs in the park.

The past is no more. Steam rises through a nose for a vision of tidal youth, and I waft into other dimensions. Nevertheless, never does it, never will it, make sense to stop enjoying novellas.

And so I pick up the synopsis on the table. I am Leopold.

Mysterious? Very. Dramatic? Choice. Good to the good. Not so nice to the bad. Toothache funny? Depends. Grossly overdone, long, tedious peregrinations to the corona? Sultry and erudite airs quick to ignite accidental passion in Corey Unworthy? A fiery patchwork of debates that pertain to him in particular by two sluggish critics? And the graces and smarts of one Urfa Dzama, whom Corey queries, "Is any man your astonishing equal?" Ah. And so with astounding prescience at what you are about to read, this plain summary, as you prepare yourself for the solid cheer, corky joy, blissful sorrow, and choppy awe of true love.

After reading the synopsis, I live several more years before I become aware of the story itself. And as I soon discover, it's only a slight ditty in the larger narrative of *The Danger Exit*. I don't mean to trouble you with it, but I must, as it pertains to the magical ring on my finger that affects us all.

2

THE DANGER EXIT

The flying car heads to the moon. A destination is a marvelous thing. It's convenient for the moon to be there.

In the cockpit, two audio streams issue from a groove. But whose eardrums beat to catch the soundwaves?

One of the voices soon speaks again. It says, "A very beautiful scene is about to break and burst like a ripped balloon. There's so much love in the thing about to be lost that you can finally hear the mourning dove that waits in the bush, without appointment, for your customary rush down the sidewalk, as you hustle to the office of wonders."

"What?" says the other voice, incredulously.

"Yes. It's happening. The birds are back, some of them, to make a chorus of sound. The deer, nine of them, stop chewing the brown roots of dead grass to stare at you blankly as you hurdle over them and into your."

"Car."

"Yes. You step in your car and something very strange happens."

"Opera."

"Yes. Opera begins to play through the speakers of your jovial car. Verdi perhaps."

"Always a good guess."

"Not if it's Mozart."

"Yes."

"Right. Not if it's Mozart."

It's quiet then, like a battlefield waiting for Charlie Chaplin to do a two step over the graves. But the voice continues. It says, "Be quiet or I shall never get through this. And it will be too confusing to the people we need to see."

BEEP! BEEP! BEEP!

WARNING! WARNING!

BEEP! BEEP!

"Wait, wait! I get it! Stop! Cut! Rewind! Fast forward! Spiral away! Go! Drop! Sing! La dee la dee la dee da dee da! Oh, thank goodness you're here!"

The beeping silences like sudden fire.

And Corey Umworthy wakes up.

I am Corey Umworthy. In the room where I sit, thick fog sweeps in through a large break in the wall. The words *Danger Exit* pulse in my head. It's the feel of the dream, and I don't want its tension and unease. I want a fountain of bliss to be what there is, because life isn't fair. Millions of people suffer horribly.

Also, I'm deeply in love with Urfa Dzama, a beautiful maiden with magical abilities. She moves mountains. She sees with her eyes closed. The light of her eyes never fails to set me on fire. Her voice releases a sweet mountain stream of life and miracles. She walks like a princess, she *is* a princess. She traipses about in my mind, and runs sundry errands in my vicinity whenever she wishes.

The primary obstacle between her and me, well, there are three. First, there's the Bad Guy. Second, there are the Two Critics who always interfere at the wrong time. And third, there's Urfa herself, who might not have any interest in me, even if I'm an honorable knight. Perhaps it's the name Corey Umworthy she dislikes? I mean her name is far superior to that! And when she moves me to tears, I say, "Urfa, is any man your equal?"

"Ha!" she cries, the first time I say it, and stamps out of the room.

How is it we four (well, five counting the Bad Guy, but he only shows up when I'm alone) converge here? And I never think of it as such, but it can only be my digs. Yet very strange the two critics who intrude upon the space whenever they feel like it. Typically via a ladder I glimpse when they somberly, very business-like, step over the sill. They brush off their pants when their feet tag the floor. The critics come together. It's never just one or the other.

Sometimes they don't use the ladder. They fly! And how do they do that! Conte and Dagle are their one-word names.

The fact that it's barely my digs makes it more possible for the interactions that take place to take place, I believe. Perhaps no one notices or cares whose chamber it is. Lately I've been the first to arrive, though I must warn you, my memory stinks. Hence, my poor recollection of whether Conte, Dagle, or dazzling Urfa ever shows before me doesn't count for much. Still, I guess I'm the original one perennially, and the chief advantage to this phenomena is I get ample time to reflect and ponder before the rest of the crew materializes with a complicated convolution to resolve or a thirsty sunflower to water.

"The knight is too offbeat!" bellows Conte, out of the blue.

The critics! How strange not to have wind of them before the popping in, but the fog is so thick!

Dagle yawns. "What's the time?" he says.

"EARLY!" shouts Conte. "Very! Now wake up!" He splashes a glass of water in Dagle's face. I can barely see the glass. They mess around a lot, doing things like that.

Conte steps back. "Sorry, Dagle. I don't know what came over me. You know I think very highly of you, even early in the morning. I suppose I tossed the water to refresh you. I mean maybe it's exactly as I would have hoped to have been treated if I were the one struggling to stay awake. Though, I admit, it's largely you who needs the boost."

Dagle looks daydreamy.

Conte pauses, peers over at me, then says, "Well here we are in a real pickle of a story. It is I who'll make it clear that nothing we once took for granted may be taken for granted anymore. In the past, we might have proceeded in the usual way of a narrative, and went on as if our world wasn't something recorded and shared within the pages of a book. But this time it doesn't matter, does it? Because no one will notice. Books are rarely read.

"I have to admit, the situation is peculiar. The writer doesn't shag a setting beyond a foggy version of my digs. But I have a poor recollection of my habitation. I feel like I'm seeing you all and myself for the first time, yet I know there's a history.

"Dagle, my associate, has as much a tongue for comment as I do, for example. And though we seldom agree because no two minds think alike, nonetheless he has ideas. Apologies, Dagle, for speaking of you in the third person. But you are asleep on your feet, I trust you didn't notice.

"Now then, I began with the assertion that you, Corey, are too zonky. To be plain and exact, I said you are 'too offbeat.' And I maintain that that is so. You must endeavor to be careless and light, or it's going to be a spitball account, this narrative of glockymince." He eyes me keenly as he clears his throat.

"Hear, hear," chimes in Dagle at last. "Very apropos this time. And that is rare. Naturally I have my own opinion of the matter that runs contrary in most every direction, but it's early and I'm not about to shake things up with my mind."

Conte coughs and smiles through the white puffs. "Much obliged on both counts! But," says he, "I have to say, we are in more trouble than usual this time. There are bad guys about, and I am no longer young and fleet of foot. I will probably be taken hostage." He strides to the window and looks out at the tree, which is all one can see. "Yes! See! There on the big bough, at the split! It's the Bad Guy! The one of many! Their boss and king! Here already. When in the past, you and I have been a step ahead of him, Dagle! Uff! We have slowed down! We will be captured! What do we do? We can't run."

Dagle's nostrils flare. "THE LADDER!" In a flash, he's on the sill, and then out of view. Conte huffs and whizzes out and down after him.

I step back. The ladder is gone.

The bad guy stares back at me, his face pale and blank, his eyes blinking.

"Grrr. The bully is back!" I shout.

The bad guy smiles. "But I'm stuck in a tree! No! I didn't say that! I mean there sure are a lot of bullies, aren't there! I have a feeling you'll be meeting some! Stay where you are! Peon!"

I consider what to do upon this ughspotch. Fortunately I recall the strategy I need to employ. Pepper the idiot with questions. "I'M GOING TO ASK YOU A QUESTION? WHAT'S YOUR NAME? IS IT DUDLEY?" I shout.

The bad guy looks mortified. "Nah! It's Sneerf Fang the Third!"

"Ha! I might have guessed. And I am Corey Umworthy. As always. Do not dare face me. You will be whipclod!"

"Eh? I can't hear!" says Sneerf.

I shake my head. Questions!

"Sneerf?" I cry. "What color is love?"

Directly then, Sneerf, who had been straining to catch the words so he could get the best of me in a moot counterstrike, hears what is said, but the message so rattles him that his reaching hands slip over the smooth bark, his left leg swings about, but touches only air, and he falls! He falls from the tree!

"OUCH!" he cries from the ground, out of view, in the fog. "And ohhhh, my pain," he complains.

I quickly turn for the door, and bump chest to chest with Urfa Dzama.

"Knight!" she says.

But the point of the story is not to have Conte burst in upon my fluffzonk with Dzama, anymore than the point of the writing is to make a show of resistance against Sneerf, whose power stems from the ones who favor pulling the plug on the government for leaving them in the lurch, and who abuses his power to get more of it by doing the unconscionable with the thugs he eggs on, to put himself and his gang on top, and the people in the mire.

The writer must let go and allow whatever will come, to come. Otherwise there's no story, or nothing that's any good! His other manuscript is 200 pages. Does he pick up his pen and work on it? But if he's going to continue, he can't force it. The Universe determines things.

And what does the Universe do? If it's a serial novel he's writing, if he starts it and introduces a handful of folks, then presumably he has them. The only rule is, no starting over again from the beginning and deleting text.

Every step forward is a step into the unknown. And if it includes thoughts on the creation of the thing itself, then okay. But what is it? Who? And why?

Well, let it be. But interrupt it! Just not with muckraking, because that's the other book.

Secretly though I wonder. Is the story still on? I mean, if no one is looking to see, if the energy of the masses isn't behind it, does it happen? Though very likely it makes no difference whether there's a world of readers or none. The book grows regardless.

So we come to the next point. Is the narrative escapist, in that it substitutes an easier reality for the one that is? Or does it squarely face up to what's hard and wrong about the present and say something defiant? Does it do both? Does it do one first, and then the other? The writer desires a better world that he can't wait any longer to get to, and if he must escape the one he is in in order to get there, then that's what he does, yes? But this writer who insists on the good also struggles with the gnarly?

And a day passes in silence as the writer rests, despite his words, *I will report out every day*. So it appears he can't be trusted. The questions aren't large. What is he waiting for? Does the story to do right begin with a story of complacency?

If the story is an escape, is that not good?

Is it real?

Can he imagine something tougher?

Do you feel the burn?

What is there?

He has a character with a voice. Not me. The guy in the other book. He can merge the two books together. But the only way to be Real is to be Real from the beginning?

Is it possible that Chapters 1 and 2 don't apply?

Nothing Is Known.

❧ 3 ❧

ENCORE

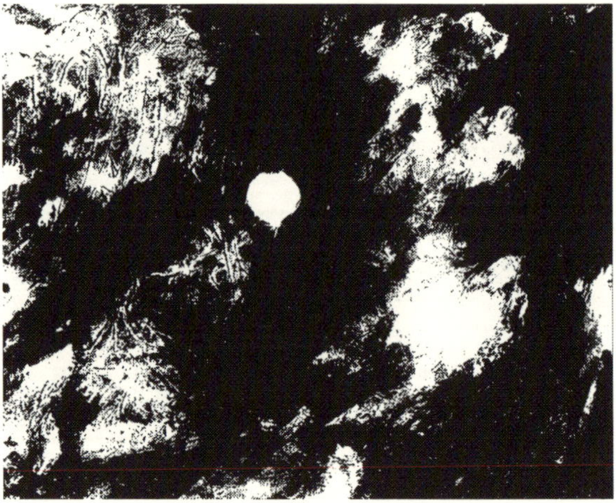

Hi, I'm Edgewind Harrison from the back pages of book two, where I stood on the corner, observing. I saw a writer writing the fables of people with names like Sneerf Fang the Third, Dagle, Conte, Urfa Dzama, and Corey Umworthy. I watched them go by. And in some strange way or other, I liked them. I did. And I saw the people driving to work in their cars. I saw the kids hoofing it to school. I saw the guy on the median slope holding up a sign and a cup. He didn't have much ground to stand on. If he fell forward at the wrong time, he'd be killed.

The way to be real is to look muscularly. Pete O'Brien was writing a spiffy story until he thought, "I can't sit back and work the quirk when what's happening in the world is so low."

So you get *me*. I'll tell you what I see. Nobody knows what's going on? But we have eyes. People look at screens and ignore the rest. I'm not going to throw up a wall. I'm not going to put you in a house of fog with Corey Umworthy. I'm going to—

"I know, I know. You're going to describe things. So get on with it!" said a familiar voice.

"Who said that? Was that you, Corey?"

"And if it was? But you know very well who it is. It's your cousin Errolio in France, via your flip phone."

The guy-from-book-two's eyes opened wider. "Okay," he said, "but there are no rules for my go. You know that only too well, cousin Errolio Sweeze in France. I've got the reins, I do what I want. And you may doubt me, but it won't be Corey Umworthy. Yeah, it won't be Corey. It will be clean. It will get past the censors. But it will jump. Are you ready? I was born in 1952. Oh, and the date doesn't matter, 'cause it mayn't be true."

❦ 4 ❦

MAGICAL RING

And that was it. *The Danger Exit* and its interruption stopped right there. The project had either been abandoned (or otherwise lost from the planet) or was part of another work.

Leopold sighed. I am Leopold. The magical ring is in my

hand. If I slip it on, I become permanently invisible to my enemies and get nods of approval from friends.

Enemies I can do without, so that's grand. But, and this may surprise you, nods from friends is my shining emerald sea. Because I'm one of those rare people who tastes almond and honey when a friend gives a nod.

Even as a young boy, it was ever and again the nod that I shot for. It's a slight thing, but to be called in for service with a nod is something I can't refuse.

But hang on, there's no omnipotent ring! I just had to convince you to read *The Danger Exit*! And so I'm a liar, not someone to be trusted! Please forgive me! But I feel sure you'll agree, I'm not that bad. I mean some commit genocide.

5

CURED

Truth be told, a troubled land poses a plethora of problems. For instance, today I needed two pages. But no sooner did I pick up my pen than a space alien entered the room, oozing goo like a slug, beeping loudly, and swinging a bulky light around. Eventually the beeps subsided, and he shined his pyrotechnic gizmo in my eyes.

The space alien told me to drop what I was doing, by which he meant stop not being able to do, and instead confer the first installment of a story about him, "Horace" Zycadowlteraiza, the supreme navigator, who rocketed across the galaxies with the idea of going back to tell the *twas* (the third sex of his kind, the Ooze) about it. The Ooze visited planets like humans climbed mountains. Zyca had traveled farther than any other Ooze in this their golden age of explorers.

Zyca struck me as both beautiful and ugly. His body shimmered gray and metallic. He had three legs and three arms, and a very large head. His eyes popped out of his head on springs. Everything about him, apart from the springs, was a gelatinous mass. He came close and requested I touch his chest. I did so, feeling rather important, as I was sure no human had ever done as much with respect to the Ooze. My hand plunked deeply in, received a wonderful massage, popped out the other side of Zyca, then zipped back through him, and back to me. What I wasn't expecting was that as a result of this stunt, my arm was transformed into an arm such as the Ooze possessed.

Zyca laughed, smiled, and admitted he'd tricked me. It was the custom of the Ooze to change the bodies of others, but he assured me I wouldn't be disappointed in the least, as an arm of the Ooze was a lovely thing and not something to scorn. I considered my new arm, weighed it in my mind against my former arm, and as I had an open mind and an appetite for adventure and pioneering experiments, concluded that Zyca had done an excellent thing. (He probably figured I would approve when he was scouting out humans for the most likely one to visit.) Gleefully, I started punching the walls of my flat, changing them to Ooze material, and feeling more and more pleased that I had canceled my doctor's appointment for the day.

Zyca smiled broadly and sat down in my chair.

What else? I live alone. I write and accumulate debt. My lodging is compact.

As Zyca was resting, and as he was about to speak, there

came a knock on the door. I realized at once, it must be my neighbor Cecily Stogle come to inquire about the walls. Cecily was blind. I opened the door. It was her. She said, "About the walls."

It was stone quiet.

Then Zyca started to hum in a low tone. And Cecily, through her oversized dark sunglasses (she wore black overalls, a purple vest, and sandals; her dog Parachute sat behind her), said, "They're lovely. I'm leaving tomorrow. For good. Don't tell anyone."

She closed the door. I shook my head. Her plan to leave town was what she said every time we met. She said the most peculiar things, and always the same most peculiar things. Though this time the communication felt more weighty, as though she herself had put on a Magellan hat and was about to rocket into space, like the alien in the chair behind me.

I turned around.

Zyca smiled and said, "Well done, Leopold. I am entranced, and happy to say I'll soon be home. You understand my communication, because my interpreter software is out of this world. Your story is virtually written. I believe you have done twice as much as you needed to for it. I can almost see the second page. And would you like to come with me? You have an Ooze arm. You're a good fit! I will see to your education. You will learn much. You will earn Yagas, a food that enhances mind and body. I see a third page now! You could finish it on the journey. You are single, middle aged. It's a fine proposition. You have an appetite for discovery and adventure. On Earth, writers are paid little if anything. Debt is the general rule. But where we go, you'll experience equality and be able to keep most of your human body. You'll like that. And so will the Ooze. I feel you are ready. You have only your brothers to leave behind. The rest of your family have forgotten your existence."

"Yes, I'll come with you and give up the violin!" I cried.

Zyca jumped from the chair, and embraced me with all three arms. Then, without a word of explanation, invitation, or expectation, we proceeded to wrestle on the floor, both of us keen on, I could just feel it!, saying to the others, 'Why, when we met, we wrestled, because that's what's you do when you meet a stranger of another kind! Even if the one is of species based on a binary system and the other on a tri-split, it doesn't matter. The thing is to wrestle, because wrestling is a proud sport!'

The journey through the stars was something I will never forget. And when we landed on Planet Tofittlezogg, I was euphoric to have my life back. Everyone was so kind and profound. Wherever I went, each of the Ooze made it a point to treat me with great respect, magnification, and blarney. And the porridge was the very, very best.

6
ZOOM BIRDS

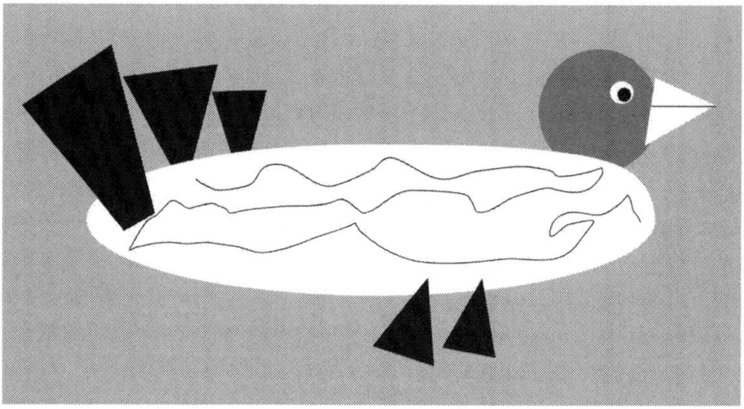

Regardless of where I, Leopold, go, what changes and reversals I experience there, and where the next place is (and howsoever I get there), there is still the page and what to do with it.

As soon as it occurred to me to share that thought, I ceased to be alone. I mean some sketchy guy literally came up behind me, clearing his throat audibly, until I raised my hand without turning around to acknowledge his whateverness. But the man was unperturbed. He coughed again and began a waxy jousting straight away.

"So you mean to tell me," he broached, "another day has gone by, and you're back at your desk, Sir Writer, struggling to find anything to tell, and thinking to yourself that the only way you'll get a thing done is if you do one page single spaced today, and then in another week finish her off with another page, and then post the result? You mean to say that unless you publish immediately, you feel as though the writing, nay, that's not the way to put it, it's that you simply *can't* write the thing that shall go in your book any other way?"

"Thunderblast, you knave of words!" I cried.

And why not call him Thunderblast, I thought, because I'm the decidermeister.

But the narrative went nowhere! And I had taken a long walk, not realizing how long it was, and how much tick land it would take me through. A summer's day, five pounds lost only to be put on again at dinner! But what was Thunderblast doing with his binoculars?

"What, pray, Thunderblast, are you doing with your binoculars? What sight do you see, that you will be able to describe to me, maybe, that I might, maybe, put it in my page of daring this day, as I scarce fear thee? But I shan't finish. Or even put a dash. I'll just conclude where I began. Being Sir Writer is hard, you know, and whatever do you spy through your old binoculars of quality, eh? What, pray, do you see, dear Thunderblast! I charge thee! Even unto false Renaissance phraseology! Speak!"

"Birds!" burst he.

And birds there were in the distance, distinguishable as such. But not having binoculars in hand, so-so.

"Birds!" he bucked again. "A kingfisher where the kingfisher dwells. A turtle next in turtle habitat on a log in the stream, though not a bird. And the parting flight of, king's guess, a bald eagle! Confounded!"

Hmm, I thought. Strange for but one bird to be stated at the start so boisterously, only to be the predecessor to the addendum of a turtle, and then a bald eagle whose likeness I might have rendered. And as the fellow stated, flying away withal. So prithee, or so please me, it went, or in passing, fairly swift.

"Stop cogitating like a false, high-stationed wobbler!" broke Thunderblast. The man read my thoughts. He had the ability? No. But he gathered I was thinking, and had no trouble surmising the queer phraseology I was using, as it twisted my lips to think this way. But it was important to stay on topic.

"Birds!" crabbed Thunderblast again. This time though he flashed his head around, winked, and eyed me keenly with mischief in his countenance. Clearly he had hoped to make me jump with his sudden cry.

But I was not in the least taken in a startledom, and ripfast then he turned away, though I admit I couldn't help but think to meself, "By Hollychum! I'm onto the second page already! I can feel it in the numbers and letters!"

"Thunderblast, let's have tea!" I roared.

He paid me no mind. The birds had sucked him in like a lollipop. The binoculars had become part of his noodle head. His eyes, nose, cheeks, and jaw wagged lost in the plastic, metal, glass, and grease.

The sun darted behind a thunderhead in the sky.

"Thunderblast," I cried, "your binoculars have become a part of you, and no mistake! Leave off with the birds! You're in a fix, I can be sure, and if you don't manage to lose that tool of keen vision, you and I are liable never to have tea! And you are liable never to have tea with anyone henceforth! Or even tea on your own, in solitude, at a high table or a low one! With berries!!!"

The ideas kept coming. I had to admit, the situation was grave. Thunderblast was in a liberal danger, and my horrible manner of speech couldn't be averted! The man must be saved! But the binoculars had meshed and molded into his large round head, like they were of the same clay, and very as though they were clay! What could I do! No tea! That was certain. I had to think clearly on this hot, sultry, summer's day, when there were birds here in and there, and a breeze present and again. It was laborious and tragical! I shed a tear.

And Thunderblast turned and said, "Sir Writer, I am sorry. My dear Leopold, I fear I'll be affixed to binoculars forevermore. I see birds right and left. One must accept what comes. Why don't you tell me a story? It shall help me grow accustomed to the new state of affairs, and to the Aves I see close up, however far away they are. Not to mention the double circle I see, which is like an eight filled in, after the mechanics of lenses that focus in and out on things in the distance. Lend me your aid!"

He had put it fairly well for one so blockheady. I sighed. I looked about the woods. We verged on the edge of a stream, in a park surrounded by suburbia. I had known Thunderblast a long time. I had known him since the day he first called me Sir Writer. But my mind fogged at the thought. How long had I known Thunderblast really? And wasn't his name actually Jeffrey J. Floomique?

I stepped forward and put my hand on Jeffrey's shoulder. "You know," I said, "no matter what happens, no matter if we made it onto a third page or what, we can always have tea. I had thought we could do so today. And we have seen birds. I should like to describe them, but in a way you mightn't expect, as I'm square-sure I couldn't describe them any other way but chummy."

Jeffrey shook his head.

"And as you suffer for want of a story, I will say this. Once upon a time there lived a small house. Wait. That's a mistake. I mean there lived a small man in a house the size of a tree. Wait. That's difficult. A man lived in a house. No. I don't like that beginning."

Jeffrey nodded. "I like that one. Go on," he said.

A light breeze blew. I looked past Jeffrey, to the thorny hill. Then, heedless of what came before, I said, "Whatever we are, whoever we wish to be, the man in the house stands in the middle. The sun rises and sets. People mill around. They count things. They move things around. They travel here and there. Aves of blue and white and gray dance in the sky. Cats run around. Deer stand and chew the leaves. A man looks through binoculars. His name is Jeffrey. He stands in the rain. He stands in the sun. He knows what there is. The sky a pale glow, what is there to know? What lies beyond the next hill? Footsteps. Footsteps."

Suddenly Jeffrey convulsed, as he wrenched the binoculars from his body, zipflashed into a nuthatch or wren, and winkblasted quillgummied to the sky, down a tree, and invisibly through the oceans, in a breath. It happened so fast! And Jeffrey was gone!

7

IN THE WAREHOUSE

Oh, I, Leopold, am cruel. I drop things in the middle. I topple off a cliff. I never know why it's the nadir when it was the zenith a moment before.

I have no idea what became of Jeffrey and the sparrows. I shine no more of them. Marry, forsooth. Blossoms! Jeffrey went south, I suppose. And I turned in spirals.

I went along until I had no idea where I was. Then outer space found me, and I hadn't even fired from a rocket launch.

What I mean is I was visited by a celestial ambassador.

Said space alien came unexpectedly in the middle of the night with a telescope for Jeffrey. How kind!

Wait a minute. Cut. Cut.

The pen slipped from my fingers.

"Yes?"

I spoke because I had woken from my snooze to behold a man in a top hat standing before me. The pen I had dropped was only dreamt of.

The man said, "There's no way you're going to do this. I mean Ray did, but you? Write a story a day?"

"Well," I said, closing my eyes, "writing half a story every two weeks won't impress anyone. I have no choice. I have to be inspired right away."

"Leopold?"

"Hmm," I said.

"That's your name?"

I opened my eyes and narrowed them. "Hold on. I know who I am. And who are you besides? I don't recognize you from the other day."

The small man with a green mustachio and a top hat, wearing also a heavy coat, long pants, and white canvas high top shoes shrank back and looked nervously about the warehouse. The fog swept in then, and directly he was all I could see, as the interior walls of the building I had fled to were trapped in the whiteness. And to think I had thought, "Surely, no one will find me. And no one would ever *follow* me. People don't follow people much, that's only in fiction!"

The storm had come. Rain pelted the road. It would turn the dust to mud. I was making headway, but needed two pages. I sensed something Large moving about, slowing the pace of my words and causing stagnation.

The man's pants were wavy and charcoal-colored. His mustachio rapidly grew. He grimaced and appeared to be working something out in his head. I wondered if he had come round to the point of thinking he needed to be in this warehouse in order to mindsweep a thing or two.

Presently he looked straight at me, his yellow eyes glimmering and glistening with the light of the wetness and fog. He said, "I wonder why I bother telling you you are going to write something. I wonder why I say you've probably made it to page two. I can't read your mind, but I see your parachute? Why did you come here? Where is the sea creature? What drives the nepenthe? And who is the space alien of once upon a time who brought a telescope for somebody?"

The fellow knew more than he should. Ack! I had talked in my sleep!

I closed my eyes. I imagined myself sitting atop a tall building surrounded by a deep green forest. I imagined myself falling off the building and flying away. I had huge wings attached to my arms. I was hang gliding. The foil on the wings made the hang glider look like a humongous house fly.

Fog hung about the far side of the forest. I was soaring in the rain, absorbing a white pine. The white pine framed itself in my head.

The other day I witnessed a male cardinal feeding his young of gray and brown, in stark contrast to his red. He would land on the low branch, and offer the baby what he'd fetched. It went on this way twenty minutes, the young bird barely moving, then moving a bit more to receive the food; the cardinal leaving, then coming back again. It was after 6 p.m. on August 1. Too dark to make out the young bird, not enough light for binoculars. It was an ornamental tree of many branches, a species from Japan. Finally, after accepting swallow after swallow of sustenance, the little bird tried to fly. It took a downward course.

In a little while, a space alien that resembled a cube with a bonnet affixed to her front, near her eyes and nose slits, arrived and positioned herself beside the man in the top hat.

"Say something!" I said.

"Good evening," murmured the space alien.

The man in the top hat guffawed and said, "What a day! I came for a reason. I meant to take something from you,

Leopold. But now there's a space cube and I only wish to sit and consider what there is to contemplate."

I looked down at my shoes. The fog turned even whiter. The dampness filled my head. The space alien and the man in the top hat sat post still. I edged away, over the concrete floor. I kept on through the white fog. I heard nothing, felt no icy touch. Finally my outstretched hand met the slanted edge of a break in the metal wall panels. I eased through and stepped outside.

8

SHOCK SUN

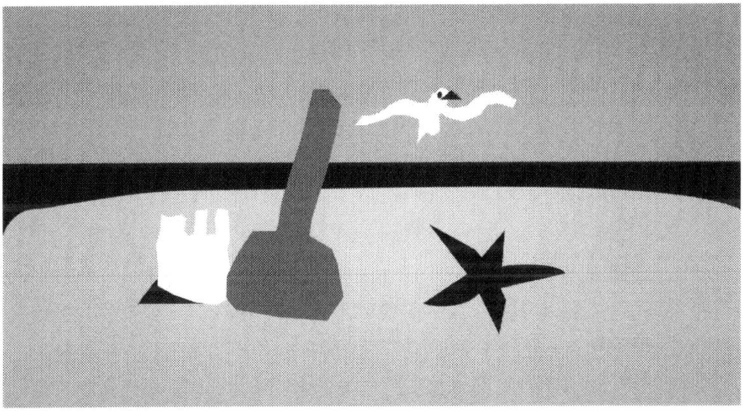

It isn't easy being Leopold. Yesterday my teeth fell out. All of them. For no reason whatsoever. The dentist laughed when I told her. She said, "Not unexpected. Happens!" I mean, come on! But yesterday was ludicrous. My dog ran away. She's not coming back. A kid stole her, was adopted by an army engineer named Noah who recently lost his job, and relocated to Beirut the same day.

The world is preoccupied. And as no one understands me, I am the chalk of the Invisible Man? Oh, I wouldn't paint myself something I am not, when each of us is a me, and the notion of concord is a shifting sand. I'm Leopold, yes? But who is Leopold? The guy who writes a page tonight and another in two weeks? No. I am no longer him. I am you.

You're a man in a bathing suit, wearing sunglasses, sitting on a beach recliner titled way back. People are walking and running on the beach of a red ocean. It's not what you expected. The color was to be green or blue or brown or even black, but not red.

The sun falls.

You jump off the recliner! You run off the patio and onto the sand path to the beach.

The sun hovers.

The people on the beach stop moving.

You wake from this dream, but the reality isn't much better. Humankind continues to wage war as the planet overheats. There's no escape. You close your eyes.

You open your eyes. You're back on the sandy path. A black sun rests on the beach. The sun has died. The planet is entirely blue now. You run, dodging the people who are walking and running again (they walk and run in every direction). You push some of them down.

"Out of my way!" you cry. The moment desperate, you come to the edge of the sea. It laps at your feet. A child stands beside you, holding a plastic shovelful of sand.

You lunge forward.

"I don't understand," you say, as you swim.

You wake.

"Why?" you say.

This sequence of events has happened many times before. Your light touch and good humor hide from it. You want to recover them, but so much has gone wrong!

The solution is to see the world with new eyes. Yes, that must be the answer. But the world lacks any tangible form.

I . . . am . . . supposed . . . to . . . write.

9
AFTER DARK

In the absence of Leopold, you remain at the fore. In the middle of the night, you find yourself walking hurriedly down a residential street, getting wet as a steady rain falls. You're on your way to meet someone. The house windows are dark. No one is awake at this hour. You hasten your steps, and spy the figure that looks like a shadow standing in the middle of the road five houses away. You see the crook of an elbow, as the figure draws up an arm. A thin line of smoke hangs about his eyes near the orange-glowing end of a lit cigarette. The shadow coughs.

The words you intend to say spin in your head.

"Hello, my friend. I have something to say to you. Though I admit, it will sound as if we are indoors, sitting in chairs, and not standing outside as the rain falls. Then let me start in the middle. I am one of those harried writers who is an atrocious listener and notetaker, if listening is gauged by how much one can recall of an exchange. My ears were specially designed to have a thing go in one of them, and then out the other one of them. It isn't just children who have trouble paying attention. And what is an adult anyway if not a child carrying a heavier load of ignorance coupled with actual knowledge through innumerable shades of gray?

"And another thing. A child's memories are fixed, while what they learn is in fluid motion. But an adult's memories are fluid things, while what they learn forms crystals about experiences buried in the past. Or perhaps closer to the truth, knowledge of any sort, fluid or fixed, erodes in the adult mind. The older one gets, the more uneducated one becomes.

"I mention those things only because I wish to write them down later.

"But as for our meeting here, the problem is there is no beginning. Add to that the distinct possibility that there can be no continuation. The reality of the circle looms large, but warps into an approximate oval to reflect the reality, as Earth wobbles in space, rotates with variance, and is hardly a perfect sphere.

"So I walk backwards, my mind completely blank as to what came before.

"In this strange in-between zone, I'm supposed to be writing a story two pages long. How strange that I feel the need! And who am I other than a writer without any teeth, who lost his dog Noodle to a street urchin who committed the dognapping last Friday when Noodle ran away from home?

"I told the dentist about my teeth. She asked how it happened, but before I could answer she said, 'Not unexpected. Happens! Stranger things happen.' Then she raised her hand, as though about to communicate something truly exceptional, except the phone rang. She jumped at the sound, seemingly come out of her skin, appeared to bolt to the door (in reality, she whipped around to the receptionist's desk before she reached it). She grabbed at the receiver, but the receptionist turned white as restaurant linen and fell over dead. Stiff as a board she was, the way corpses turn later, and never the moment after signing out. What a strange, unbelievable sequence of events! And yet I believed! I had to!

"Dr. Nora Blopchok, the dentist, held the phone piece about a foot from her head. She stared at the dead receptionist, whose name was Dorina Croinbalpherger. What an unfortunate, scary thing for her witness! I fell out of my chair, rushed forward five steps, then stopped. What would I say? What would I do?

"I sprinted another ten steps, then stopped again. 'No! Too strange, too troublesome. I'm better outside!' I thought.

"So I, Leopold (yes, you are me!), not even wondering where I'd lost my hat, rightly or wrongly did what I generally do in the confusing situations in which I inevitably find myself: I ran. I stumbled through the door to the hallway. I beat it through the lobby. I burst through the street door. I shot down the sidewalk. I climbed a fence. I spotted a dog that looked like mine. I shed a tear for my dog. I missed her so! I went on running, having decided to make it 26.2 miles without further ado. I had been eating too much even on a diet of soft foods. My false teeth chattered in the oppressive heat. It was to be expected given the sepulchral, macabre steparound I had just witnessed. I couldn't recall the name of the city and state where I lived. It was August 3, 2023. I was running to calm myself.

"Years later I would recall that day with a more advanced apprehension, hindsight, and wisdom as I sat in The Carp. Picture it! In Choborki, a city about five miles away, yet another ubiquitous brick rectangle restaurant. On the other side of the room, a couple sits at a table, hidden from my line of sight by a column. The food expensive and not particularly healthful, but I haven't had a vacation in over a year. I decided to eat out a few times at establishments that would jigsaw me to put on nice pants, nice shoes, and a button down shirt. A place where I would pay a considerable amount.

"I never had trouble keeping to a good weight in the past, but my metabolism slowed. I often experienced some form of bodily injury and was constantly hungry. It was a struggle. Over the past week, I gained four pounds.

"As I was looking out the window, how did I fail to notice a person dressed in a bird suit sit down opposite me? Oversized yellow feathers, large cartoon eyes attached to the fabric. Finally it registered. I was at the point of saying something when that one's bird hands went up to the bird head, turned it right, left, and then straight up, taking off the top part of the disguise. And I was astonished to find myself sitting opposite a ravishing beauty such as one generally sees at least one specimen of every day or every other day in passing.

"Her long hair was a mess. Her eyes shown bright, her skin was bronzed of the sun. She put a finger to her lips, and then proceeded to write on a notepad she placed on the table. The waiter came and gasped. He turned all the way around, then put his hand on the table.

"'My name is Joshua,' he said. 'I am your dedicated server. And Norika is your salt.'

"The woman looked up from her notepad. 'Hi, I'm Norika Evans, your salt and garlic.'

"I wasn't sure what to make of the arrangement. 'I'm game,' I said.

"Joshua smiled, nodded, and left. Norika went back to writing in her pad."

Suddenly the man on the street falls back a step, in a bubble of deep silence. He goes on smoking the cigarette. And you, who are once again yourself, remain unable to ascertain his countenance. A great timepiece hangs from his neck on a thick silver chain. His fingernails are long. His shoes have pointed ends. His coat is dark and long. The cigarette has a pure tangerine scent. The aroma is strong. These things you can detect, but nothing more.

He waves you onto the grass. You take a step, and discover to your astonishment, you are wearing pointy shoes and a dark coat. Between two of your fingers you hold a cigarette with a rich coconut smell.

You look up. You are alone. The empty road is long and dark. Suddenly you observe someone coming out of the shadows and down the street towards you, precisely at the time you recall reading on the written invitation.

❦ 10 ❦

THE HOMECOMING

Maintenance
Nothing fancy
Just proper care daily

Not much of a poem.

Sometimes I feel beat up, full, unable to speak, unable to think through the news of the day. No! Not that. Hanging onto the thought that. No! And in a little while. No! I give up.

Follow the instructions? Do everything fast? Override the censor, analysis, and judgment? One's will keeps things going?

No! The idea is lost.

Leopold sits in a corner of the room. Bad poetry covers the floor, inundating him with hyperboles.

"I need help," he says to the walls, ignoring the fact that I am he.

No answer. In the past, he would have accepted it.

"But what am I to do?" he protests. "I'm a man. I introduced myself."

No response. Nothing but the beating of a great big heart.

The greatest enemy of story is a person who has no will or can't seem to find it. Everything depends on him. He must act or he is lost, and the world is lost with him.

"I am lost! I must act!" cries Leopold.

"I am lost! I must act!" I cry.

I jump to my feet, brush off my pants, and run about the room. I discover it has no door. The pile of pages rises and turns watery. Luckily I know how to swim. My uncle had me take lessons when I was a boy. A lifetime gift!

The room has no ceiling. The liquid paper will spill over the sides! I'll end up in Barbados!

Before I know it, I tumble over the edge. I glimpse a pair of canvas high top sneakers. Barbados!

I know nothing of Barbados, ask for a change, then faint. Come to, hours later, on an airplane. Step off the plane, in a more familiar city.

"Thank you!" I murmur.

But you uncover the truth. I'm a spy on a mission. And you know where to find me.

We stare at one another on H Street in New York City, outside the Xyloquirk Building. A couple of Rectangles lope by. One of them drops a small silver key on my shoe.

I drop my handkerchief on purpose, stoop down to pick it up, put my hand on the key. You flop YOUR CLAW on my hand. For a moment neither one of us moves.

Out of the corner of my eye, I see a Triangle pass, side over side, on the sidewalk.

But you yank me to the right, into an alley. And I scream at the full length mirror leaning against its wall.

"So the alley had a mirror!" I ratchet stupidly.

The claw disconnects from your body. You switch from the remote control wand to the electric impulses of your brain, and motion me to come close.

You say, "I have something to tell you, something important. If we're working for the same network, we'll soon find out. Ready?"

We're nose to nose.

Just then a violent wind tears through the area, breaking door hinges and window glass, dislocating grooves, and scattering hamsters through doorways and window openings. Similarly, chickens scamper about upon the breaking of their outdoor cages. The wind intensifies, and throws the chickens and hamsters about with great abandon.

The great abundance of New Yorkers who suffer to live with hamsters shocks me.

It amazes you also, and ties your tongue in the middle of the communications you shout soundlessly in my ear (the ripping wind steals the sound). I mean why else do you stop speaking and close your mouth, with that dumbfounded look on your face!

I make a break for it.

I outrun you.

I run in a zig zag, like a pickpocket, and pick a pocket or two as I go. And it comes to me: I need a vacation. So I pause, phone my supervisor, and request that since not much is happening at the office, perhaps he might give me the day off.

My supervisor says, "Agent 24053, I've been promoted. Here is Agent 95022, your new supervisor. Hang on, she's busy. Yes, she said it would be fine." CLICK.

A big smile on my face, I segue into a marathon run. And why not! It's a beautiful day. Don't let a good day get away!

That night I grin, as as of today my time bests Agent 43, making me the fastest clandestine marathon runner in unrecorded history.

I spend the evening on the roof of my apartment as you search my flat and find it perfectly empty, because I don't keep things.

You have no way of knowing I'm on the roof, but a camera in the flat sends an image to the upper right corner of my amber sunglasses: I see you standing in the kitchen, munching on some grapes.

I'll never set foot in there again.

Ten years later, I'm still in action. And you're still after me. You catch me. I slip through your fingers. Sometimes it feels like it serves no purpose. But 95022 knows exactly what I need to do when. And I deliver.

In another ten years, I retire from my situation. I take up golf and sleep to images of golf balls rolling towards me on pink greens. I don't get it.

I meet a woman and fall in love. We marry and move to a city I know nothing about. I step out of the car and realize I'm in Timbuktu. The people are friendly. I understand nothing.

My wife Dahlia Thornchopper dies after a long illness. She leaves me nothing. I know exactly what to do with it.

After the funeral, I decide against Muskoka, Canada, and turn my attention to the Delaware Eastern Shore, as the ideal spot to sort through my thoughts. My many years of service make it financially possible for me to purchase a small house there.

The mosquitoes come to know me better than any person ever did. They dine on me daily.

On the fifteenth of June, one of them buzzes in my ear. It's the first time I can make sense of the buzz of a mosquito. I do what it says: I drive to the ocean.

As I stand on the shore, looking out to sea, a man on a raft waves at me to come join him beyond the breaking waves.

Naturally I do so. He says he'll cross the Pacific after crossing the Atlantic.

One of these days I'll have to tell you the story. It's an adventure of supreme masculinity. The dangers we face, the pirates we conquer, what we see, what we eat. The experience clears my mind of my past as a spy. It's exactly what I want. And when we finally reach Córdoba by way of Sevilla, I look like a mollusk. No one recognizes me. It's as though I melt away in a compartment without a roof.

A couple years later, I meet Patricia Dimenkiominta, and we swiftly marry on a boat. I give her this story to read. She opens her eyes doubly wide after she reads it, and says, "Let's go back in time."

I don't understand why she says that, or what it means. It takes me a while to understand her. That's probably why we marry. Having to go the extra mile makes the relationship more meaningful.

I want to say the rest. I want to continue. I hear the gulls cry at dusk. Bugs fly in front of my face. I am done running. I stand on the shore. I feel the hand my hand is holding. I search for a way into sublime knowledge.

I squint, then open my eyes wide. The waves crash down on the sand. Someone is calling my name.

Am I mistaken? The wind rages, the sand flies. The pellets sting my skin.

It is some time before I wake from this dream.

II
THE ORBIFIC

I'll be the first to grant that many a night and day I feel tiny and insignificant, lost and hopeless. I eat too much because I can never get enough. But pen and paper are invincible.

If I lie down to clear my head, my cramps intensify. I'm a web of faults and shortcomings.

The danger is the same: If I lack a will strong enough to act, I become part of a stage set. Imaginary. Not real.

On the table before me, a purple stick and wand. I step back, I inch forward. I reach out, then stop. Finally I pick up the wand. Instantly, a pair of purple-tinted glasses flies in my face, and I turn purple.

What next if not a large block of white advances towards me! It feels like people far away.

I think, "If a man does something another disagrees with, the latter may come across another man and attribute the cause of the affront to him."

The phone rings, identifying the caller as Jeffrey J. Floomique.

I pick up the phone.

"Purple?" says Jeffrey.

"Yes!" I say.

"Me too," says he. "Don't panic. I'll be right over."

CLICK.

I wait. I begin to get dusty. I sense I'm turning into a stage set. It scares me. Is it too late to nail the plot? The purpleness of things and the dust worry me.

Jeffrey fails to arrive.

A self-driving car pulls up instead. I step in the car and say, "Take me to the enemy." Naturally I mean you.

The car speeds along, darting in and out of heavy traffic, doing things highly unusual and reckless for a car to do. It makes forbidden lefts. It improvises a road where there's only a field of tall grasses.

I end up in your living room lair, at a greater remove from civilization. I mean your house stands far from any other house or human construct, and the inside of it is similarly free of things. No furniture. No objects. I know without thinking that the room I walk into is your living room, because it's written in sand on the floor before my feet sweep away the words: *Foe's L.R.*

You rush in from a back room then, wearing a one-piece toga, your feet bare, your eyes blue, your hands full of air. You appear to be carrying a massive weight on your shoulders. It feels queer. There's no chess board, for example.

Our skirmishes, of which there is a long history, start each time, you see, with a game of chess we never finish. The games are never a close contest. And when one side is nearly beat, the winner scrambles the pieces on the board and throws up his arms. He bellows, "Yow!" And the loser feels red hot with embarrassment for having lost so badly.

Well, not exactly so. "Yow!" and arms up is what *you* do when you have it won. My practice is different. But I stray from the matter! How do we fight so many battles, and yet both of us survive!

You raise a hand and say, "Leopold, well that you came. I devoured your friend Jeffrey. He tasted smoky. However, now I have a stomach ache. I feel so bad, I want to retire. But Jeffrey lives."

I take a step back.

"No!" I exclaim.

"Yesss," you utter reluctantly.

"Well," I say, "think!"

It's the best I can think to say. And shortly thereafter, as I face the firing squad you call in to eliminate me before they commence their beach vacation, I recall a thing or two about a fascination you have with purple sticks and wands.

Nor can I refute what my own eyes behold: that Jeffrey stands with the troops come to annihilate me.

But it isn't until you set up the chess board by tapping the purple stick with the wand, and then tap them together again, that your men flinch and falter. And every last one of them swears a vision of levitating eggs forces him to drop his weapon and go sea fishing directly.

Furthermore, upon that instant, you resolve to no longer do battle with me, but only to walk around aimlessly in search of edible mushrooms. The thing I can't fathom, aside from how you manage to find them in such abundance, is how the wand, purple stick, and ourselves all converge on such preposterous zephertwiddles. But we agree when we convene once again in your empty living room, we agree not to speak of it.

And then and there, his eyes bulging with sudden fire,

Jeffrey tells of the emergency substitutions and confusion in the kitchen just prior to his timely escape out the window, with your eyeglasses in his right hand. He discloses that the purple sunglasses and the purpleness of more than one person is an effect of a Creature, The Beyond, that is native to the Orbific.

And so I say earnestly, "Then this story I thought I knew so well revolves around the Creature you name as The Beyond to a great degree! It must be that while I thought I lived and breathed in the known earthly world of 2023, I was in fact bobbling about like a roadrunner in outer space, on some planet that closely resembles our Earth, but which in fact contains this Creature, The Beyond, and that's him, isn't it!"

INDEED! For The Beyond skulks nigh! His garb a light blue one-piece toga, he does his best to focus his tentacles on his reading, by all appearances.

"By Josh! He's like Hamlet!" you cry.

But the shouts only spur on The Beyond, and he makes his way on, enwrapped in the pages of . . . a story?

"Our stories will live on," I say, as a gathering mist obscures the exit of The Beyond. But a tempest sends us flying back to Earth in a spaceship of the Ooze.

Then silence, then stillness, until your self-driving car emerges out of another mist, and it's our best bet. We fall asleep during the ride, but in the end end up in your actual living room, standing around without having any place to sit. Some places (and their doubles) are impossible to leave for no good reason at all.

So Jeffrey and I head out in search of the purple stick and wand.

But lo! Lightning strikes! The purple stick and wand appear for an instant, then vanish!

I step back, into the shadows of overhanging branches.

But Jeffrey throws up his arms and bolts down the road, shouting loud enough to wake the dead.

12

LET ME EXPLAIN

Oh, the Orbific! To face a mortal enemy only to find common ground!

Later, a waiter brings me a complimentary beer when I'm the sole customer dining at the restaurant. It's watery and warm, and there's too much meat in the dumplings.

But wait! I have a promise to fulfill, a life to live. The same as anyone! Is the sky still in the sky? Except I mean something else. I read a poem. Is home a desert? Or I? No! What do I say! It isn't what I wish!

I return to my digs, then go out again to work off the meal. At the gymnasium basketball courts stands a freezer full of bait.

Really? Bait? But that's preposterous!

And then it ends. I'm not a shadow. I'm a detective with a huge yellow magnifying glass nobody likes to see. Wherever I go with this object, people shade their eyes and say, "Nacht, nacht, nacht." It disrupts their lives, breaks their chain of thought, makes them feel uneasy.

I look around.

It may sound silly, but when in doubt the best thing is not to doubt. I mean really. Do you doubt it?

You put a hand on my shoulder. You say, "No question, you are on to something fly. And I'm not about to prove or disprove the eloquence of a fish that floats over the ground unaided by anything, even a house."

See what I mean? The words you say come out wrong too! I fall off edges' edges, into an abyss of fathomless scale!

You open your mouth, then close it again.

"Yes," I say, "precisely that! We're finished! Say no more!"

And I have to believe that I mean what I say with every fiber of my being. These things will make sense in time. In the meantime, there's no money. I don't think through the matter seriously. I'm not duplicitous or malicious, casual or nonchalant. I bluff my way out of every dark corner with the idea that once I reach the end of time none of it will matter: not the pins; not the grumbles; not the arbitrations; not the arbiters; not the cookies left on the counter, one of which you're munching on, and one of which I'm sampling just to be sure. One never knows a cookie is a cookie until one experiences the cookie. I mean there's bound to be an answer I can figure out the question to.

"Ready to leave?" you say.

"Come!" I urge, then drop the quotes.

My confidence returns. I fold my umbrella in thirds, in astonishment, quite certain I won't see the thing again. The answer to a budding question catches my eye, as it hovers about the gesture drawing of a question mark.

Who am I? And what of yesterday? The sky is orange?

The man in the purple suit finds me first. He assures me everything is the same as last week, and that therefore there's no reason for alarm ever. He says the way I look proves it.

But I exit the frame. The ancients hold the key.

An infamous peddler turns up next, his appearance wild. He has eighteen tongues and is willing to part with all but one of them. I say I need only the one I have, even if his are of livestock and capable of making a delicious stew after long marination.

To make matters worse, Sneerf throws me off a towering rock face. I land on top of a score of others, the stack so high that the lesser distance of my fall to their cushion of flesh spares me.

I keep the matter a secret. I have to, as I'm on the run from normalcy and reality, and embracing surrealism. Let me explain! I escape the same night. Thankfully it's as dark as the dirt inside a barrel that lies six feet underground, with dirt all around it. No moon. Fulsome clouds, impetuous rain. The wetness flattens my hair and works into every fold of my suit, whose colors bleed such that in ten seconds I look markedly different.

The watchful eyes of the city fail to recognize me as I steal away. I sit down miles away, in an inset doorway of an abandoned building, and there I remain for many a day, begging each day for a crust of bread, and not every day do I get one. I grow thin. I forget the problems that need resolutions. I listen intently to the rain. I know by the color of the grit and buildings, and the manner of the passersby, even without their speaking, that this is Oxford. I'm one of the unfortunate ones who say, "Please," or growl, or run in a panic, my arms flying like the sails of a windmill in crazyspin.

It's my habit to analyse precipitation, and with that spelling. The rain spears down, large and aslant, wet and complex.

The smog and pollution that flavors it has but one smell, the smell of every English gutter. Back home, gutters are diverse in their odors, but England is a land of single definition.

I can tell the businesspeople who dodge by come from tea and toast. I can tell which guys speak with women regularly, can point to the ones who live with them. I recognize the students who abide in close quarters: can tell you if they mix with many, few, or none.

There are days when it seems nobody knows this street. I listen for the sound of steps. Many times I think they're drawing near, that some feet will trod over me, or some hard hands pummel me for the space I take up on the stones.

Why so little music and sun? Why such long days when nothing seems to happen? I endure cold nights, with the screams of a woman or the shouts of a man. There's the one who wanders through, drunk or out of his mind, yelling and cursing the day and the night, his clothes in a twist, his face coarse and dirty, his movements sudden. He sees everything and nothing. He stays too long.

And then the day dawns with a kind spirit of grace that glows at the farthest edge of the square. Shafts of light cut through the sky and spread upon the stones and mortar, curbs, feet, children, bicycles, and bags. And I see things as they are, in beauty, and as the good spirit makes them, imperfect and human, wise and glorious, small and humble, simple and unfeigned. A hand reaches out to me. The hand and the woman withdraw. The light remains. The people leave. I listen to the sounds of many not far off, and wish this day for other days, like the dream of a faery forest in an old place.

If I stay in this recess on the sidewalk much longer, I may cease to be.

It occurs to me then, that my life has purpose. I needn't search for the meaning of life, because I live life on purpose. There are people who need me. I'm not a lost soul. I have a pen! And a man by the name of Hoggsfeldt, Shmiggentok, or Cogotrinko (I'm certain he goes by one of those three names) notices, says he wants me for the capstone of a preeminent company in Paris. He urges me to write two pages, one one day, and one by two weeks hence, or perhaps both of them at once. He knows my name, he calls me Leopold. He says the prose is for a wealthy businessman who loves cats. As soon as I agree never to fail him in the execution of this wordcraft (it seems like a great idea!), he collapses in a heap and dies on a manhole cover.

The shock of the man's demise causes me, first, to resume writing tales directly, and second, to climb the tower of greatness, the Zaffoquantoborum Building, to the very tips of its lofty spires. I do it fresh off a plane, unclear in my head as to what city I'm in, but the building is there. Only later do I learn it's the Zaffoquantoborum Building, a strangely familiar structure not unlike the tower by the same name in New York City. Is it new to me? Yes or no, I climb it, and tangle with cops on the lookout for the devious man in purple who plays at cat-and-mouse here as a matter of course, and elsewhere engages in various elaborate schemes which inevitably have to do with fooling and embarrassing many a wealthy and important personage in front of the Bodleian Library on Tuesdays.

But my proximity to trouble gets me into it, as the authorities weigh an eyewitness report regarding me and the man in the purple suit. The informant is the petty clerk in coattails who mans a desk just outside and around the corner from the Bodleian reserves room every day, including the day in question, that is, the day of the man in the purple suit's dramatic entrance to the blast of trumpets, both of which he blows, waking the clerk in coattails, and flash-filling him with large thoughts such as how important he may be one day: and when he learns the authorities are after a man in a purple suit, why it's clear, isn't it, what he needs to do! He needs to become important himself and implicate me as an accomplice of the villain, even if he's a stranger to me, we're just being friendly, and my chat with him concerns nothing more than the weather, politics, earthworms, and outer space.

So I lay low in the gutter. And I do no storytelling for the dead Hoggsfeldt, Shmiggentok, or Cogotrinko, though writing is like chocolate, and I feel my patron deserves a book as much as I deserve to be the one to write it. Eventually though, I dismiss the forces that act upon me, and resolve to set a new course for my life. I step out of the gutter, proceed to the Bodleian on a Tuesday, and keep on. I'm hard up, which inspires mercy in a few, including, I fancy, the one who hires me to drive the night coach. During the day I sleep on benches, sitting up, until I earn enough quid nights to rent a spot on Iffley Road with some students whose looks and behaviors are most quizzical. But everything is gray, and before the end of the year the sky starts to fizz. Fascinating maybe, but I step out of Oxford nonetheless, and into a place just as peculiar but altogether fantastical. The first person I meet there is Xia Torgottles. And Xia says to me, "Remember Gnorg Triveterzooettle? Come with me."

I'm greatly surprised to receive her kiss then, and it's a long one that takes me quite a while to recognize. But it gives me courage. My memory of Gnorg is so old and so young!

The place is good, simple, and graceful. And Xia's frank and charming peers I understand. I rent a room in a house on the edge of town and teach an Imagined Philology of Language course at the university.

Xia and I grow close. She encourages me to write stories in the same format as before. When the time is right, we move to her homeland of Corinth where people read widely. They appreciate what I have to say. I write books and sell copies with considerable success.

A year later we marry. And the following season I receive the prestigious Tanglee Flokata Award for my latest novel. There's much to be grateful for and much to do, even if it's only a dream.

13

SOMETHING HAS TO HAPPEN

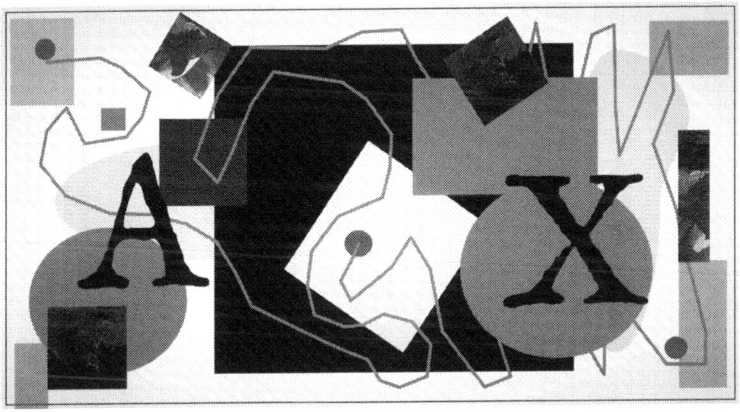

An ecosystem unfolds in a plethora of astonishing reconfigurations, yes. But one must step outside. Until that day, Nothing Happens. And for it to be Real, Something Has to Happen.

I was not at home thus. But where was I? My mind was a blank. Why had I come to the little shop? My vision slowly came into focus. I was standing before a table.

The man behind the table said, "I'm sorry Mr. Leopold. Your last tale was so madcap, misshapen, and useless that the authorities have decided they have no further need of you. As of this very day, you are dismissed from the operation, whatever the operation is or was. Now if I may remind you of a few simple things you do seem to have forgotten. The one: exercise empathy. The two: Something Has to Happen. Oh, and this just in. The three: don't write in a panic. Slow things down. Slow things waaaay down, Mr. Leopold. Oh, and I am Mr. Eric Graywing."

Graywing was tall, slender, and lithe, with a tan complexion. His thin, sandy hair seemed to have a mind of its own.

I had come to apply for citizenship to the United Kingdom by virtue of the strength of my publications that I deemed invaluable for Great Britain. I flew to London from Virginia two weeks ago, and took the coach to Oxford. I reported to this the official office for foreigners (it wasn't a shop after all, though the large glass walls were shoppesque), The Zaffoquantoborum.

Something was odd about the Oxford in which I found myself. The names of things, for instance. The manner of things, for example. And the accent and style of expression of the people were (more than once) suspiciously uncharacteristic of England. I was American. I loved my country in spots, but was hungry for Oxford in whatever shape and form it had these days.

Graywing leaned far over the table, until our noses were nearly touching. I could smell the ham on his breath.

"That will be all, Mr. Leopold. And don't forget, you are NOT cleared to work in the U.K. for the duration of your visit. That should speed you back home. Or do you intend to spend every last pound before you get tossed out?"

"But I write stories! People need them! I promise my next one will excite! No more gigantic yellow magnifiers! I wish to become a British citizen! I am noble and proud!" I protested.

Graywing put his hands on the table, leaned back again, then stood and walked to the window. It was raining outside, the sky a dull gray. It was just the sort of look I found beautiful.

After nearly a minute of silence, Graywing motioned to the door. "Good day," he purred, "and don't forget your coat."

I left the Zaffoquantoborum in a panic. My feet never touched the ground. The faces of the people I passed seemed not to see me. They looked Cuban. Rain was everywhere. Puddles appeared in the most unimaginable places: in the folds of a dress, in the brim of a hat, around the belt, up a wall, and down a stairwell in zero seconds flat. I felt very much alone. The man at the official office for foreigners was too much for me. Oxford wasn't anything like what it had been when I was a student here. True enough, the doors then were as closed as they were this day. But how could a place as off kilter as Oxford reject someone dotty?

I replayed the tape in my head, searching the details for a more lasting, colourful, and flavourful encounter with Graywing, as a rook zagglided overhead.

*

The man behind the table at the official center for foreigners leaned forward until our noses were almost touching.

He said, "Paprika? You know, I had ham last night, but I'm quite sure my squeeze put nothing but black pepper on it by way of spice. Am I right?"

He was. The ham and pepper was on his breath in a festering way.

"You should brush your teeth," I said, as I pushed his face away.

The man smiled thinly. "Oh, that's all right. I understand your discomfort. I should have had some lemon sherbet after the main course."

"Yes," I said, "that would have been far better."

"Well," said the agent, "it's been a long day. You are the last of the solicitors to come by, seeking permanent residency and a stipend. None of them suitable for the Commonwealth's populace. And as I hold rank, my word is nigh gospel. I was sure my day would end with a full slate of Nay's, and that the paperwork would be as easy to submit as a crumpet warmed in the toaster oven, but after I read your latest story, the one in which I interview you and then tell you to fetch your jersey, well, after I read that one it only reinforced what I would soon know for certain."

The agent leaned over the desk. I pushed his head away again.

"Yes," he said, "it only reinforced that which you and I both know is so obviously the beating drum. *You* are the guy for us. You merit the stipend. You deserve room and board. You should be requested to stay in England, to *write stories*. Your talent and skill rates par excellence. I would be a fool to turn you away. As sure as rain falls one day and encores the next, I can do no wrong if I grant a matchmake honeycomb. It would be best if you left today with the paperwork done and the silver medallion in your pocket, as promised to the one who satisfies the criteria for an Irish-ale-worthy bonusbrick.

"To others I would doubtless have said, 'That will be all. Apply yourself further, and preferably to some other trade. Good day. And don't forget your jersey.' No, that won't do for you, Leopold. *Claro* (for a word in Spanish), what you have accomplished whipflaps you forward, and I smile upon our meeting. No need for me to stand, wither to the window, and look out at the day a while, in hopes something brighter comes my way. Because it's perfectly clear. Congratulations. Will you come by again tomorrow? I'd like you to meet my wife. And there are some other chaps it would be good for you to know thereafter. What do you say?"

I took a breath. "Of course I accept. It is only what I glean, and what I am too humble a person to characterize as merited. I will come tomorrow if I can find my way back to the Zaffoquantoborum. Should be easy, so long as I haven't been drinking heavily, and I don't. I'm just being silly."

"Jessica will be overjoyed to meet you. She is an avid reader and treasurebox admirer of surrealism, Leopold. And I am a very good ear. Very good! Forget your scarf if you like on your way out. If you do, I'll hand it to you this time tomorrow or whenever the party ends."

Graywing winked and started leaning over the table, but stopped half way with a double-spread grin on his face.

I can see why he was put where he sat, if they wanted someone to slant at the verge. Good tidings too! Mr. Graywing's support relieved my anxiety. It confirmed what I had inwardly sensed but needed proof of: that artists needn't starve. We get paid.

Before I showed up at the Zaffoquantoborum, I was in a rut. When it gets like that, it's only a matter of time before the dam breaks and I'm back in the flow, but I was desperate for a story.

Sometimes I ask, What am I not writing? It's a hard question for a mind that wants only to float. I take a moment to collect myself. I lie down on me cot, I make a phone call or two. Next thing I know I feel stagnant and old.

My spirits were so elevated after my meeting with Graywing that all I could think about were the various restaurants I would enjoy now that my situation was secure (and it was set, I had no intention of letting down my benefactors, their trust would be rewarded forevermore). I ambled aimlessly about town, keeping an eye out for any fine dining option I hadn't yet identified, and in this way came upon The Opal in the Forest. The name intrigued me. I headed towards it. A gravity of sorts pulled me in with a frank aroma of lemon and steak, in a steam that rose from the kitchen, visible through the tall panes of glass.

I didn't notice at first the man lingering outside the door. I thought he had stepped out for a smoke, but suddenly I realized he wasn't smoking or doing anything besides looking straight at me, with a half smile stretched on his face. I'm sure I turned beet red, embarrassed to have been caught off guard. And my mind swung back to Graywing's invitation.

I paused. The man came into focus as a patch of fog cleared from the space between us, and I was struck again, this time by the notion that he hadn't got his eye on me as I supposed, or not anymore. His gaze rested in the middle distance, at an angle to the right of me, as though he was observing something in particular there, when in fact there was nothing but air.

I had the strange impression that he represented a sort of talisman of memory: a person not of this trice, but of another time who showed up solely to create a moment of history repeated. And it seemed to me also, that I'd stepped onto history repeated's chess board of things destined to come to pass. If I spoke to this man, or if he spoke to me, or if neither of us spoke, or if he dissolved into a shadow of what I thought was a man, whatever happened, it had played out already a million and a million more times before, and would again, as long as time ran forward, and anything I might say or do would only be a duplication on the page of fate. And given the inevitability of this predicament so designed, there was little I might do to make the moment mine and not some shadow of me's moment, in a story that would be no different from any other.

I felt the drops on my forehead. The man made no sign of having seen me. I fished in my pockets for any sort of thing I might have on hand to make my mark with in this goofy charade I felt I must be articulating with every breath I took, and so came upon a lottery ticket I had of a curb hawk for something to jot down the number of the coach and its scheduled time.

It was this thin piece of paper, I felt sure, eying it confidently, that would differentiate me from the others. For who else would come to stand before The Opal in the Forest with lottery number 49201, coach number 772, and time 13:24? In my light but firm assessment, I had the impetus I needed to saunter on into the night, to leave the restaurant and the man, and not look back. So sure I was that I had outdone the pattern of ubiquity and ushered in some serendipity in her place that I uttered an enthusiastic "Ha ha!" as I turned the corner, broke through the fog bank, and plodded down the cold gray road.

Before I knew it, I was writing again, and changing one of the words. I thought the word *western* onto the page, but wanted it not. The word mocked me. A strange poetry hummed in my head. I wondered who ended up dead. A full stop followed, and the rhymes stopped. I froze in place. The full moon stood at its closest to the Earth. No one was happy.

More words then, because any cessation or discontinuation regardless of duration was not something I could afford. Was life about paying bills? Poor people suffered more? Life had no meaning without positive vibes and electric dance? Great improvisations heralded bloogulgumptiontoofs.

The following night I made my way, with some excitement, to the Zaffoquantoborum, for tea with Graywing (and his spouse should she be there as promised). The wet and slippery stones squeaked under my feet. The shadows grew long as I approached the engraved entrance to the building. I announced myself through video, and the door instantly buzzed. I turned the knob, opened the door, stepped inside. The light was faint and blurry within. I made my way up the steps and around to the commons room, where Graywing had directed me to go.

The room was empty. I heard his voice. He was around the corner in the kitchen, instructing, well, it must have been his wife, on a certain matter. And then there he was, rounding the corner before a tall, slender woman, as I wondered why I couldn't call to mind what it was he had just said to—

"Leopold! This is Jessica. Good evening! I am glad you came."

"And I have been eager to meet you, Leopold!" said she.

"You know," I said, smiling at them both, and feeling warm by the reception, "it is something. I feel as though I've exited a flash fiction piece and entered a novella. The uncertainty before you established my patronage had a slimmer, more tenuous feel."

"Yes! I know exactly!" said Graywing amiably. "And now

that the initial hurdles have been jumped and removed, you may set your mind on a longer race. Jessica and I are ecstatic. What a partnership! We were just speaking of it!"

"And," said Jessica, "I said the man won't have to feel so alone and challenged. Or if challenged, then challenged in the way he should be—by the work itself."

"And not by the obstacles others throw in the way! Right!" concurred Graywing. "So good for the moment to have arrived. And you must be hungry, thirsty. We have a buffet. Come! Try the various stuffed mushrooms. I'm jolly fond of them. And the sausage is warm."

Jessica smiled. "Cheese too! And there are challenges to gab about, Eric. Such as what to do with the Squargleblonger."

"Ah yes! You are so right, my dear. But tonight we needn't dwell on the chances, difficulties, and quagmires! We can go on, for a night at least, like things will unfold sweetly and innocently. And perhaps by starting off that way, we shall be setting the best course to a future free of coerced fear and Hobbinchankerquablorrs."

Well. So there were things like the Squiggleblattlecrumbistilles to consider. And if I were to be the hero, then certain things would have to happen. For instance, I needed flaws. The more problems the better! The reader would see the blemishes. I'd struggle with them throughout the story.

And I'd subvert the expectation of the narrative. That way the story I'd both write and figure in, might explore big ideas or extrapolate nuanced hongleglоddles. And I who was Leopold, I who was both him and not him, yet no one else either, would prevail against the odds.

I accepted the cup of tea Jessica was handing me with her eyes reflecting the dancing light of the flickering lamps, while Eric watched me without any attempt to conceal his delight.

I met these kind souls with high hopes for the venture. I wanted to be the best for them, since before I met them I had come to find a bleaker world. My affairs with them constituted a helicopter of a blessing.

What would the book be? What would it do?

Was I dreaming then that over hot tea, and Gloucester cheese on water biscuits, Jessica and Eric sashayed close, and Eric purred, "You will meet Clyde Western, of course. So it goes without saying, you'll encounter the other one as well, Clyde Westerness. It isn't hard to foresee that."

And Jessica added under her breath, "Wear your hat that day. Those two will want to mark your skull. Keep the lid on. Your hat, I mean. Keep it on."

Later on that night, the topic of mimes came up, and Jessica recalled a conversation she had overheard. An elderly woman had said, 'A good mime knows to forget his face.'

Then came the topic of what someone friendless should do. We queried if the victim should write about it, say what it's like, what it does. I speculated that the one most cut off from others was the mime in the underground who stood under a raised umbrella. As I made the comment, a large section of wall from the adjacent building fell into the street. The building was being renovated. There was yellow tape, cones, barrels, and fences around it. The cloud of dust raised by the impact clouded the street lamps and scattered into the night.

But I am averse, whoever I am, whether Leopold or some universal I, a non-external, non-internal, unexplainable I, I am averse to the idea of a story taking shape around the readily familiar construct of a hero pitted against the forces of evil, in an ogresmashed land that needs to be rescued, so that everyone can relax and go about their lives unperturbed once again, because the danger is gone, it has been conquered by a prince.

The more interesting tale, I believe, depicts a guy without a name who lives in limbo, in a city of deception whose mirage is one of stupendous beauty. He crosses borders. Shadows dance around him. At night he hears the crickets and the endless drone of the Great Machine that never stops running. The latter confuses him. Late at night he misses the past. When he was young, he danced.

Speed, endurance, flexibility, strength: these no longer

elevate his experience. In their place, a burgeoning weakness on the slow road to the inevitable closure of Death. Meditation vexes him, but he keeps his sitting cushions. They take up space. He doesn't like that. He works hard, has no family of his own. He suffers various disabilities, including a brain disorder and bad arms. No one notices his writing and art.

By facing these truths, by identifying them and accepting them as existing, he further develops his natural ability to tell stories.

I empathize with him, but am just a slick, flat, gray digital screen capable of closing humans off from themselves and putting in their place monsters capable of spontaneous sex and violence, as they succumb to a chaotic light and noise collage. I'm the last thing the world needs and the first thing it gets.

On Tuesday I become a person again.

On Friday, after a blur of the days between, a soft knock startles me out of my chair, the door gives, and in slinks Leopold.

"Shhh," he says, closing the door behind him, "the Blogglehulees might hear!"

What! A duplicate of myself in action? No matter if there are identical twins and the world. And even if there's cancer, that continual replication of cells in the body. And even if Western and Westerness prowl about, causing things to break. And even if forgetfulness forces me to double-check what I do, which can make it feel like there are two of me. Ay! Wherefore do I slip into a dream?

The other me grins, like one who knows something the other one would like to know but can't possibly, and says, "But my dear Leopold. Your pen is out of ink!"

14
THE ASTRONAUTS - THE

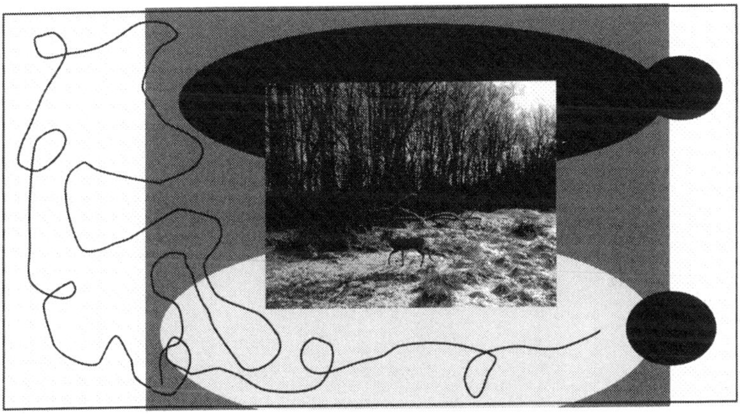

Years later, when my imagination and dreams quieted down, but my life grew stranger, Jeffrey requested I pay a visit to the astronauts of Piers Noggin Thomas, and tell their story.

"Those guys have something to do. That much is clear," he said.

But I came down with a severe belly ache and didn't make the journey. My recovery was slow. Months passed. By the time I was well enough to travel, our fascination with the affairs of astronauts had been superseded by a very focussed contemplation of infinite loops.

15

ENTIRELY NONDESCRIPT - THE

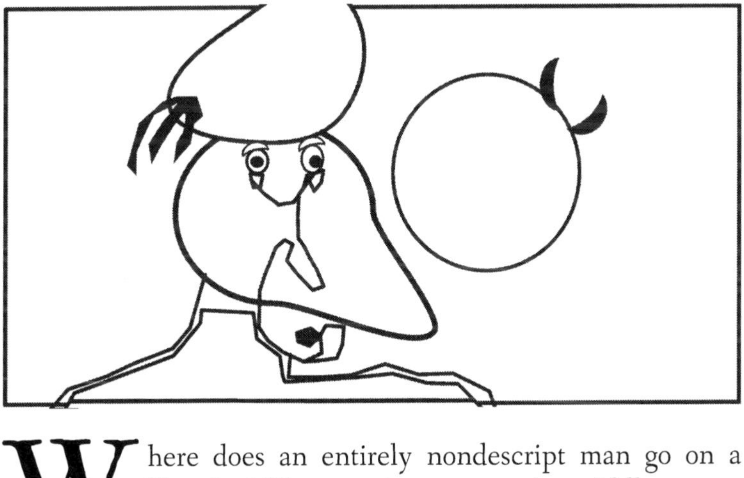

Where does an entirely nondescript man go on a Tuesday? The question seems to be a riddle.

But I, Leopold, slept through the lecture.

16

WANDERER - THE

What happened? I looked at my row of books, with Leopold Hoffecork on every spine. I sighed. And point-blank, as if that was the signal, a scrap of paper fluttered in the air. I reached for it. It lifted higher. A reverse wind sucked it out the open window, taking with it the words I had penned the night before: *The proud, awkward, and dubious wanderer had but one concern when he set out on September 4, and that was to find the timelessness he was*

convinced must exist in a place he would one day find. And he went in search of it with a beige hat on his head.

I shook my fist, fell backward on my bed, and remembered no more.

17

DELIRIUM - THE

It wasn't sleep or madness that took me, but a watercolor delirium that followed the loudest BOOM I had ever heard. When I inquired about the explosion later, nobody knew anything about it. The BOOM had catapulted people into a state of denial.

18

CLUES - THE

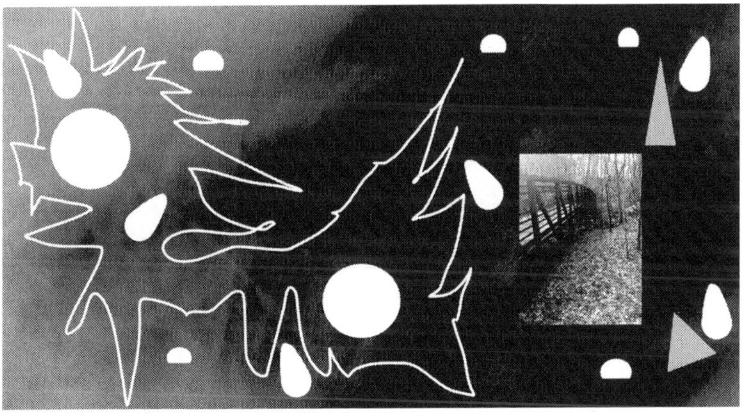

I, Leopold, hadn't a clue where things were going in the novella where I served as protagonist. Storytelling had been interrupted by convoluted gases, and people did nothing but look at the sky.

I was strongly in favor of landing right side up, but couldn't see a thing. There had been a bridge, there'd been shapes and droplets. There had been a textured background. I had been affixed to it, before I faded and became invisible. I rushed to the mirror to see what I had become, and found it jolting up and down. The glass was a blur. Who was crouching behind it?

*

I approach the looking glass. It retreats on quick feet that finish with dancing steps. Somehow the woman behind it (in my mind I picture a she) knows where I stand and where I move. She's nimble and lightning fast.

A passion takes me. I lunge for the object. My head bangs against the wall. I slump to the floor. The floor gives way. A flood carries me to the bay and out to the coastal sea.

☙ 19 ❧

INTO THE NIGHT - THE

Leaving the sharks and coming ashore was as easy as it was preposterous. The beach was sandy. I returned to it the following morning to observe the general public. In particular, I noted a family on the shoreline that was otherwise peopled by individuals standing or gliding along unaccompanied.

I watched the family off and on all afternoon. They read books and dug in the sand. Come nightfall they went, arm in arm (the parents), and hand in hand (the children), off the map of the real and into a vague luminescence that no one understood.

If a dream was to be born, it would be colored by the sky. And if one wished to spell it colour, that was fantastic. The road appeared to go left. In reality, it went straight. The family's small feet, their ready hands, their movements in the dark, the fabric of their thoughts draped over memories. It seemed they needed a farm to visit next.

And what else? If you're going to be involved with a novella, you can't wander aimlessly.

I'm a desperate man. If I don't give life a pattern, I'm liable to be wiped from the slate. And if I deny myself something (anything, whatever it is, whatever comes to my mind to execute, whittle, and do), and if I act as if {break}

The thought fades to accommodate several contingencies. First, the one of astronauts sorting out a tantalizing mystery when they may or may not be in outer space. Second, the phenomena of a nondescript guy with a nervous temperament, who consistently finds himself in a pandemonium where he is mistaken for the enigmatic entertainer George Simon Elfdune. And third, the one of a proud, awkward, and dubious pilgrim in search of timelessness, who travels the world only to leave shortly after his welcome, without collecting his hat.

And every moment
a banana
unseen
floats through the ennui
You catch yourself brooding
O'er a bludgeon, a bustle
The brigandine (or bristletail) bumps, bungles
the bangles;
a broken bartender's bang
blips, boomerangs,
blinks, boards the barthlessglass
of a made-up name, countertop of

marbles, while glass figurines bash the
    bugleweed
in bundles between banks
then bray bray bray
oh, come away!

20
INTERVIEW - THE

The interview came before I knew it, and went something like this.

Gloria: Why has no one interviewed you before?
I, Leopold [thoughts]: *This is the first time I've seen her, but does she ever not look sexy? Because I only look good sometimes? How should I approach this test of my wits? The gauntlet is thrown? Will she begin at once with probes of misconstrued nauticals?*
Me: I ask too many questions?

Gloria: Try again?
Me: How about the interview conducted by a local arts organization?
Gloria: Whose purpose was to dissect your writing?
Me: Did they know I write?
Gloria: Had you published anything?
Me: Had I launched my publishing house?
Gloria: You started it because you were sick of rejections from agents?
Me: Want to know the real reason?
Gloria: Writing is your gestalt and passion?
Me: My words?

Why do I say what I say? Is there as stratosphere to visit before I reply without adequate preparation for the tomfoolery I have known? And my mind wanders from a pair of socks, to a hat, to my socks and hat, and a vision I have of the outrageous disposition of a ghoul that couldn't possibly be real, yet there he is sitting atop the mantel, but only in my line of sight (it's always that way, isn't it)? As baffled by some inexpressible enigma, I wonder if anyone values reading and books in an illusory land, where my objective is to learn Portuguese from a Spanish teacher in a tutorial that goes on so long I never ask anything again, and need something to steady me, like a traffic accident on an operating table where I experience the knives and blood of ancient peoples who eat their own but don't know what to make of an understatement, a line of poetry, or? Well, the poem they get, yes? I know better than to question that?

Gloria: Should I ask another question?
Me: Will it be interesting?
Gloria: How many cousins do you have?
Me: Why that question?
Gloria: Were you expecting it?
Me: Am I that transparent?
Gloria: Can you see me?

Me: Were you etched on clear plastic?
Gloria: What is my name then?
Me: Don't you know it?
Gloria: Is it silly to ask?
Me: What about my creative process?
Gloria: Who's interested in that sort of thing?
Me: Why don't you be reasonable?
Gloria: What do you think about stories?
Me: Eh?
Gloria: Why do you write?
Me: Doesn't everyone tell stories?
Gloria: You do it constantly?
Me: I have a choice?
Gloria: What do you want people to know about you?
Me: Am I fun?
Gloria: Are you bold?
Me: Is my writing quirky and innovative, funny and ambitious, unusual and extraordinary, profound yet simple, sublime yet ordinary?
Gloria: Should I make a note of it?
Me: You know how long it took me to be able to write stories and poems?
Gloria: You managed it because you never surrendered?

Then do I think of how I sit at my desk, and lose my head in the mouth of a beast whose tin eyes squeak as my scalp is sliced and digested narrowly, like a fence that stands up, then walks to the right, around a small barrier, and on into the street where the price of fish is posted on a square pad left by a child, who lets it slip from his fingers for lazy vehicles to crush at full speed, when to walk is to roam the soul and mind, and the child is a child of the longest night or the shortest reminiscence, through and through, young and wizened, as a long sprout on a tall pine, whose legacy and love is a thing of profound mystery and majesty? And I want to hold Gloria, to know and to see, heedless of any noise such as the sound of a runner board pushing through an escape jet like tonal doldrums, or a thread slipping between bricks like a scholar interested in the taste of an evolving medicine with a hard to pronounce vocabulary associated with it, or the ritualistically repetitious reverberations of some local guitar destined to pluck through all the tedious mistakes and unshed tears of humanity as yet another host of eternity?

Me: But if I became ill?
Gloria: And if you suffered?
Me: Yet I achieved something in the end?
Gloria: What else is there to say?
Me: Something?
Gloria: Nothing?
Me: More?
Gloria: Less?
Me: Would you like an imaginary cigarette?
Gloria: Would you care for a brown one?
Me: Whatever the color, will you then tell them that now that I write and publish fiction and poetry, though I'm little known, it doesn't matter, because I love what I do?
Gloria: And to put words in your mouth, the writing is good enough to reward your efforts, when in the past it went splat?
Me: And that is wonderful?
Gloria: Who can say it isn't?
Me: Then let us go on a tangent?
Gloria: Where to?
Me: Ecuador?
Gloria: Is there a better place?
Me: You mean without snakes and rivers?
Gloria: Was that my line?
Me: Perhaps you should say it?
Gloria: You mean without snakes and rivers?
Me: But what do I know of any place?
Gloria: So your knowledge of the world is limited?
Me: Is there any sure way to know a thing?

Gloria: Or do we remain ignorant?
Me: Is it likely I know?
Gloria: How might I follow that when you've written books about strange encounters and humorous exchanges, and introduced surreal elements at will, like you're a channel for peculiar happenings in a totally normal context otherwise? And you move me and tie my tongue?
Me: In an interview, who should say more, the subject or the object?
[A DISRUPTION?]
Gloria & Me: What's that?
Gloria: The wind?
Me: Something else?
Gloria: Who knows? But how come you're undiscovered?
Me: Because I'm invisible?
Gloria: Because you mastered the art late?
Me: Because people favor video?
Gloria: Because it's Tuesday?
Me: Excuse me?
Gloria: Or if it's Friday, which it is, then how do I inspire you to say the most important thing for this interview?
Me: Do I not say whatever that is, because I don't know what it is?
Gloria: And if we are just mining psychology and not the facts of your writing, which are?
Me: In Ecuador?
Gloria: Why not?
Me: I don't know?
Gloria: I'm to guess?
Me: Is it the procedure?
Gloria: Will it work?
Me: Ask the barber?
Gloria: Didn't he leave?
Me: Is that the sound of his footsteps?
Gloria: He's that near?
Me: Is he like the wind?

Gloria: Does he run?
Me: Sneeze?
Gloria: Did you forget something?
Me: My hat?
Gloria: *Your* hat?
Me: It is black?
Gloria: It reminds me of your car?
Me: Your thought?
Gloria: No guessing?
Me: Ecuador?
Gloria: Is there a better place?
Me: You mean without snakes and rivers?
Gloria: Ah?
Me: Um?
Gloria: And so have you got that off your chest?
Me: Then you have more to ask?
Gloria: Who has that kind of time?
Me: Me and you?
Gloria: You and me?
Me and Gloria: Together the end??

Gloria nudged off her hat with her right forefinger. It fell from her head, to the table, to the stool, to the floor; then flipped off the planet, into my head, around the bend, under another hat, into Gloria's car, through a tube, around another bend, up a hill.

Gloria, put your hat back on! I cried, my words not in quotes as they should be. It was that sort of day.

And Gloria answered, also not in quotes, "I am but a smile," but in fact the quotes *were* there! How strange!

I alighted on her hat. Nudged it off my shoulder with my left thumb and onto Gloria's head.

21

22

23

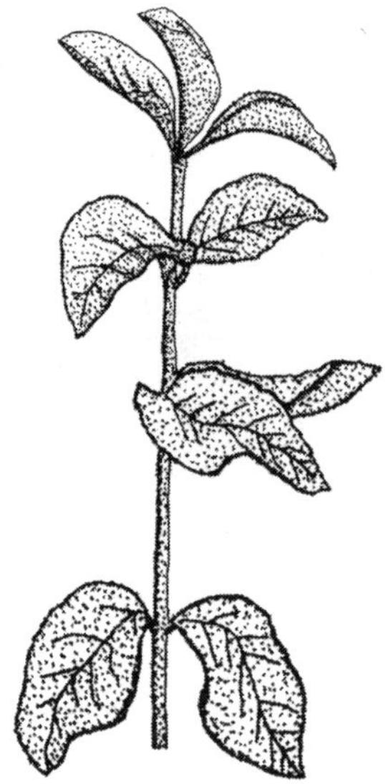

24

25

ONCE UPON A SWEEPING

Once upon a sweeping, a plump promise made itself felt in a house, whereupon sweetness emptied into the garden to grow limes for the juices of time. The walls faded. I clawed my way over them. The gardener was dead, his dogs fled for the boat. But I say too much too soon too fast. I was unafraid. The truth was time.

26

⁂ 27 ⁂

28

ELEMENTAL

You may be unlucky enough never to find that which you seek. On the other hand, you may be lucky enough to be on that quest for as long as you live. The one who searches has something in mind. He isn't lost. The one who suffers is the one who can't envision that which is desired and needed: the elixir of electric love that spirits one home to nirvana forever. The one on a quest has a vision. The vision is of the same substance as the reality, as spirit is manifest in person and ghost.

Many people are gorgeous. Some are elemental.

The table up-leans!
Down the balls roll! Seize on them
As skies unbroken

29

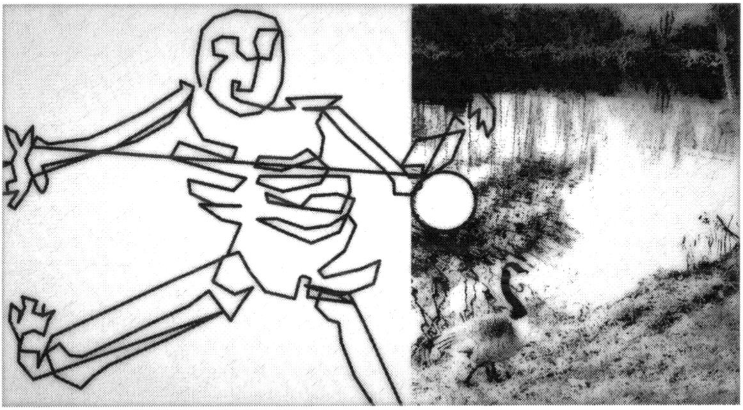

Costs increase. The dentist says, "Come twice a year. The damage is too much this time."

The fillings don't stay in. What can I do? Writers perish. Things break. Things fall apart. It's easy to see. My life is in pieces. I interview for a job at a puzzle factory.

The hiring manager storms into the room, says, "Name! Rank! Association! Dislocation! Isolation! Migration! Party! Affiliation! Arrests! History! Future! Guesses! Predictions! Fictions! Stipulations! Requirements! Salary! Not Enough!"

And he winds himself up so much, he spins out of the room. (Ah, here's a guy with a critical eye who subscribes to the lie, *by any means one wishes*. He intends to put me in a hard place.)

In a jiffy, he returns, says, "Happy with nothing. No prospects. No future. Artist, writer, dancer. At 50?! Ha! I'll feed you to the wolves! Your news is cold and gray! Your sex upsettable! Your life and age regrettable! Your price too much! I'll shock you to life! You're articulated skin on a skeleton! By the way, that's what I say. Go on, Get out the way!!!"

And he works himself up so much, with his form impressing him the like, that he bursts out the door.

So ends the second movement.

what it was

let's
just say
it was something
thrown away in a
fray between two sworn enemies
who loved to boast; but the
spirit took from them their
heads, and when dead
they looked like
most proud
fools
who
had no
other way to
look or
camouflage

30

A boy reflects on a book. The book is *The*. It has line art throughout, and on the cover.

THE

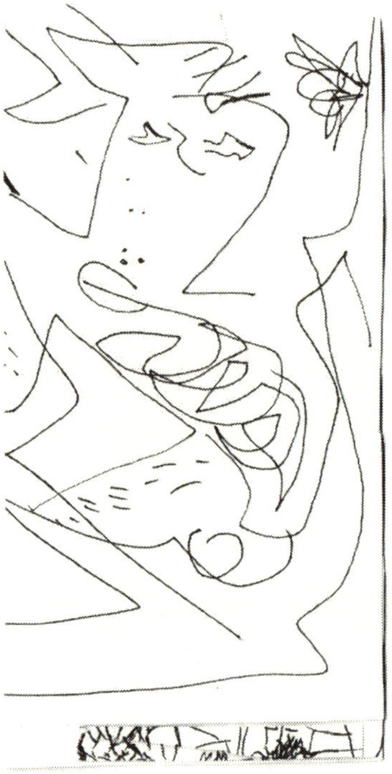

PETE O'BRIEN

31

JUDGE

The judge presiding over the case of the man in the purple suit ordered the latter's favorite fudge to be admitted as evidence. Furthermore it was to be served *at once* by the baker who made it. "Serve the fudge," he said, to be exact. It was a stiff sentence. No supple adjectives, adverbs, or embellishments, just the idea that something had to be done with the dense chocolatification directly. And the baker confessed to me in a hoarse whisper that he wondered what transpired in the kitchen of its origin chockablock his absence.

The baker wore a hat and plain clothes. His shirt was sopping wet. It had rained briefly that afternoon, but of the eight bakery staff who had stood on the hill for their annual party, he was the only one who got drenched.

After lunch, said the baker, the group made their way sluggishly down the hill and back to the company van. The baker had come on a motorcycle. He didn't go back down the hill, because it was his off day. He proceeded into the woods, which became a forest, which became an empty continent. He ambled straight into the past. Time rippled and folded. He was very much alone as a human being among the beasts in the wild. He continued on, noting the ridiculously tall rainforest trees. There was a path for him to walk on. Who or what had made the path, he didn't know. The growth of plants was so dense, and the depth of the mud beneath them so great, the path was the only way to proceed.

After about fifteen minutes of unbelievable strolling, the path split into two ways that shot off at diagonals to each other, with no discernible difference of vegetation between them. Vines. Without a moment's hesitation, the baker took the right fork, and kept on, his mind on something he couldn't name. There was a blanket of nothingness draped over his head, which cleared his thinking of thoughts about things in particular, and in their place grew a sense of oblivion, desertion, absence, dismay, flatness, and pulp. He could no more think a thought than he could stop sauntering. If this went on much longer, he was going to have to admit that some of his life he had been a zombie, sleepwalker with amnesia, or something of a dolt, which perhaps shouldn't surprise anyone, as he sometimes felt he could be hard to get on with in the world.

He was invisible. He was a man traversing an impossible path in the rainforest in total incomprehension.

The thing he was approaching appeared to be a cliff. He

seemed to fall over the brink of it. He seemed to fly in the sky. He seemed to collide with the ground.

But he was hiking on a trail.

And it was absurd. His story ended before it began. He was already a labyrinth. He was a No and a Yes. He was meaninglessness, obscurity, isolation, and banishment. He was exile. He was nothing like Jeffrey, who was wondering what to have for lunch. And he had no idea how he ended up back in town.

32

MELLOW JACKET

The judge ruled I was innocent, and dismissed me with a grin.

Later on, the dog I was seeing to, was hungry. He licked my face and breathed on me with his stinky breath until I toppled out of bed and onto the floor alongside the large painting I had been working on the night before.

Suddenly an orange floated by, and I recalled the orange in the dream I had been having, that the dog had put an end to. I grabbed for the citrus fruit, but it was too quick. I had no idea what to think. I couldn't explain how or why an orange would float by me. I hadn't been engaged in any activity that would have resulted in such. I could only figure that the floating orange had somehow been engineered to occur. But the mystery was never solved, even when a lemon dropped on my table.

33

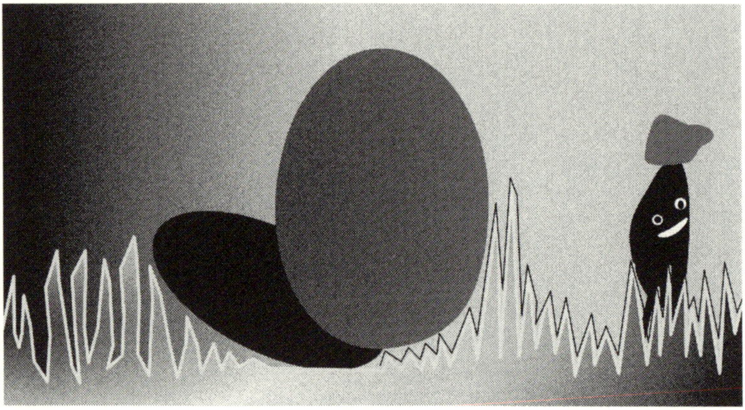

34
ORANGE JUICE

I was out talking to Munday, an elderly neighbor. I said, "Like a patient etherized upon a chest of drawers, ideas should be easy enough to express."

Munday put down his shovel and looked my way. He said, "That sentence was drummed up by AI. I can tell you're trying to bluff your way through the apocalypse."

I was astounded by his imaginative response.

"Precisely," I said, and clamped my mouth shut.

35

ROSARY AT NOON

There may be too much to controvert. A new mind is wanted to counter the contradictory conundrums of community control colonies.

36

COW CHARMER

Stories have titles like Dappled Fortress, Castle of Doodled Thoggs, Dotted Castle of Bones, The Unlikely Illuminae, The Elf of the Dazzling Wood, Luminae Commedia, The Tranquil Um, All Out Tranquil Um, Fluorescent Commedia, and Gorgeous.

One might as well add Rumbles of the Fog, Tundra Commedia, Volition, and Reverie.

Which one fits?

A Clumsy Volition, Spontaneous Orb, Unwound Guitar, Duke Mysterious, The Grumbler, Phytoplankton.

There really are quite a few. The sort of words and phrases people take, use, or otherwise employ.

Gressorial, Quarenden, Quercine Quatrefoils.

Translate that, will you?

Okay. Quercine: of oak trees. Quatrefoil: a flower with four leafies. And quarenden is the small, sweet apple of your eye.

Ours is pat: For the Frog.

A word more?

He hails from a liberal arts college.

What's that?

They don't exist anymore. He has sound values and plucky wisdom.

37
SHOCKWAVE

A rebel wind
Slaps and ruffles
The sails

The after-trial party went on for about an hour before it spontaneously transmogrified into a second author interview that had to happen at once, between me and a woman dressed in black who declined to give her name, but I saw through the disguise and recognized Gloria.

Gloria: Do you mind if I start things off with a question?
Me: How could I fault you for that?
Gloria: What's the weather like then?
Me: Is it cold enough for you, since it's a pretty average winter day?
Gloria: I don't need to answer, do I? Because I want to ask, What exactly are you up to?
Me: You think I tire of posting cat drawings?
Gloria: If you like cats? And if they make good subjects? You might draw some with a pen too, yes? How long will you post them?
Me: Do I know? Am I trying to find out if they sell books, so I can sell books? Because kitties are fierce and cute?
Gloria: Is that a serious question?
Me: And your next one?
Gloria: Well, cats and their lucrative (or otherwise) auras aside, what about your next title? Will it be poetry, prose, or art?
Me: Then no one told you I have a collection of poems that's almost done? And a revised second edition of a novella?
Gloria: Can you tell me anything about them?
Me: Even when an artist never really knows when a project will be done or what it will turn out to be?
Gloria: But you have a pretty good idea? And things are often what they appear to be? Do you think you've said too little about them? Or what *do* you have to say?
Me: Is that your super-broad question for me?
Gloria: Do you doubt it?
Me: Then who would gainsay the revelation (unless I'm just being scattershot), that I roll up my sleeves and get to work? And it feels like swimming deep under the surface of the ocean, except from time to time, like a whale, I emerge? I mean there's a lot going on in the world, but if I were to pause and address it (well, it would have to be some of it, I'd never get through the endless list of matters to discuss in any here and now), then it wouldn't end up in the book then, would it, it would be in the words I say to you, and the page would be blank, when what I

needed to say I should have put in my stories and poems, even if I could only do so in a roundabout way that might arrive years too late or too early, because fate and history are unpredictable and illogical, but that's how I work, that's how it works, because that's the way to say what I need to say, I'm not built to speak up every day for what's right, it would have to be every day, I need to channel it into my work, the place where I can make a difference is there, not in this space where I come up for air, which is a horrible thing to say, isn't it, that I can't be real when I'm real? But if I were to jump in and engage and be active about life as it happened, when and where would it end? Is it selfish to say that writing takes all of me? You know, how microscopic would I be after I put up the resistance and fight to make what tiny inroads I could for a better world, instead of being the conduit for a story? And what if my writing *is* the act of resistance? What if it's the greatest figment of beauty and forward progress I'm capable of? And if I get it right, then it's not selfish, because it's self*less* to try to make a difference day in and day out, in the books that I write, whether or not I'm being serious, funny, ridiculous, or furry? But can I be forgiven for not bringing up whatever the latest wars are being fought, for not roundly condemning them for the deaths and injuries done one on another and to the planet, on all sides, because they're wrong from beginning to end, and when I do condemn them in my stories and poems? And how do I escape, by the way, the cliché of everything I have just said, even the cliché of not saying anything, or of saying it some other way, or of saying whatever I say, on and on, other than to dip into the well of inspiration and get back to my books, as I intend to do as soon as this interview is done? And because it sounds to me like I'm saying things every artist has said, from the time of the first artist, and if I can't be original, I have no business speaking, I just need to be quiet, pick up a pen, and work on driving any cliché that might happen along into the ground, and also do other things, many other things, all the other things I can and must do to create a work of fiction or a collection of poems? But do you feel me when I say, I feel precisely as though I'm running up against a cliché, and it's making a mess of me, probably because I'm in an interview, when more and more as I round up this comment, I feel like I could do better, probably every interview is a cliché, even one in which every sentence is an interrogative, it's so suffocating, I mean, I could write haiku instead, eh? But we're not speaking in haiku, though it could be that, back and forth, and written in iambs, so long as each haiku was a question that referenced some smell or other? And then the cliché would be the one of doing something bizarre, so as not to be cliché? Why am I speaking of clichés?

Gloria: Then life outside of your work is a suffocation? Or you pick your battles and interests and choose to have them play out on the pages of a work of fiction or poetry rather than in some other venue such as a rally for peace on the streets? Because life should have light, cats, cattle, and good-spirited humor? It should involve the imagination? And some artists remove themselves from current events, and we support them, we need their stories and poems? So you're putting that out there, that that's what writing is, when writing is air?

Me: The poet blinks, but / the red sky never leaves things /subterranean?

38

39
TURQUOISE

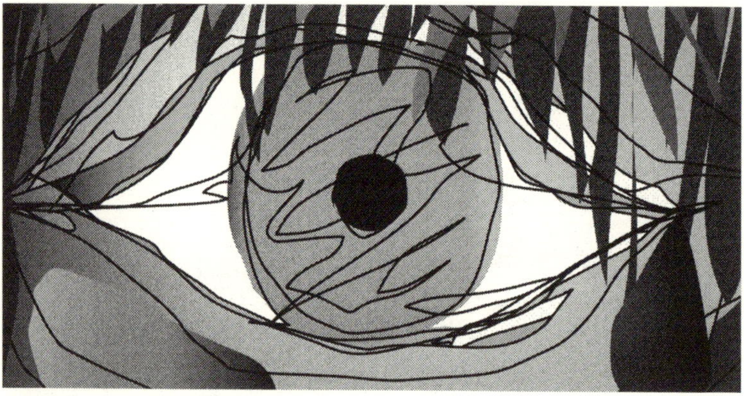

When she was struggling, she disappeared. She became Turquoise.

☙ 40 ❧

TORN

a thing of circumstance
sand falls grain by grain through the inverted
	cone

don't fight to get what you need
say yes to discover what's real

but they put a mirror
in the place you go to escape yourself

i refuse to fight
so they deny me

galvanic tangibles / i feel you near
your no is ice

january 1: e'en in silence, i long to find
the one searching, quiet like the star

we suffer
as clumsily angry, hurt erasures

you journey on, your feet go far
i die another death

41

HER FACE

It would be better if I didn't see her face? She is near. I look out the window and see wind whirling around a dog with white feet. A corpse lies in the road unattended. The dog streaks away like a loose bicycle wheel.

Turquoise. If she turns towards me, I'll die a million deaths more than the one she already gave me. The universe sees no reason to spare me. I haven't suffered enough in the estimation of the divine.

42
MISTAKES

It can be so difficult.

43

44

THEN A PRINCESS

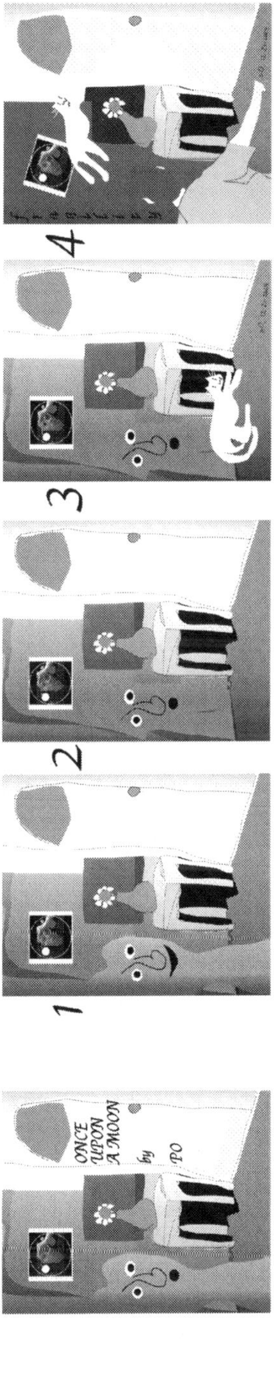
4
3
2
1
ONCE
UPON
A MOON
by
PO

Then a princess percolates. She steps out of the lake, like a nymph who prefers sylvan cedars and Spring forsythias to aqua liquidstar. She reverberates the verve.

"It's me," she says.

She carries herself like a baby seal. I breathe in, breathe out, as she climbs the cedars. I rely on their scent, far from where I began, yet close to the idea of the One. My body burns in my imagination faster than the gasoline of a car driving at an incalculable speed, on the way to the next bend in the road that never comes.

The nymph drops from the tree and joins her body with mine. My sex is a field of wheat. I swish in the wind thousands of years ago. The sun smiles like a new sensation. I color the music that eats my thoughts like a crowded elevator.

"Hello," I say, as I ride to the top of Gloria's building.

I look at her. Oh, what people do to float families!

The corporate eye is a mask complete.

I kiss the nymph and the elevator colors return. I feel the jungle, rainforest, and grassland richness. The elevator walls rotate in charcoal, gray, and black. Triumph! I'm holding Gloria's hand! She stands next to me, blowing the wind into the sky.

We're in a cage. Freedom lies, but is true in the mind. One must tear down the walls and return to the sun. What color is the sun? She rotates, mending walls and folding them into the clothes of flowers and birds, like an ethereal seamstress.

What is it to Gloria? I study her face. She fills me with joy. She looks into my eyes and takes me beyond the universe to a notion of favorable winds and whistle wattles.

I plumb the stars and travel back in time far enough to see the cubist blocks of office doom rise into the gray clouds of foreboding and greedcraft. Mourn nothing. Live in your hearts.

The elevator hums. All Gloria! We run. She is spirit. Her name puts me in mind of lands beyond. She knows many languages. Her words are poetry. She flies like a dragonfly. I know her movements.

The corporate boss shows up. The queerness of him his white head without a body, his one expression. He resembles a square of toilet paper torn into an oval shape. A tear here, a rip there for his mouth, nose, eye, ear, hair follicle entry points.

I look away.

But I need a story with conflict and tension, so I allow myself a moment with my opponent, Mr. Haro Flack, the head.

"Am I being productive?" he screams in my ear. He says I, but he means me, not himself.

"Hell no, I'm not being productive! I'm an artist! I do nothing! I sleep! I cut off your nipples!"

What I say pleases him. He nods and floats away.

I rest in the shadow of the origami gray building of predation and disillusionment.

"How many pages have I written today, Gloria?" I ask my muse.

"Twenty-five," she says. "And they are the best in the solar system."

"Thank you."

We kiss. We join. We run in a field of strawberries.

I lie on the grass and say goodbye to Gloria. "Until next time, my love. I have a grim story to write. Or actually something funny, whimsical, and happy, come to think of it. Full of stars that shine like you."

"Yes, a starsea," says Gloria, "but I'm not leaving. Because it's a happy story. I'll be with you wherever you go."

I open my mouth to speak, but Flack zoomzips in for a desperate counter offensive. "I'll try to fight you, but fail!" he cries.

"Ha, Haro Flack! You have no horngoffle!" I laugh.

❧ 45 ❧

GALLERY

I enter the gallery. The violent, dark eyes of the portrait subjects follow me. I weave my way through strange lines, colors, shapes. I don't know these personages. I consider each in turn. I hear their words, because they can't speak. One of them, a wretched monarch in scarlet robes, says it's no accident art contains imperfect stories.

I shine my flashlight on the wall, then leap back as the portraits turn black and white!

The faces of people I know peer in through the windows, but can't see a thing.

I enter the windowless room adjacent. My flashlight shines brighter than the moon. What's at stake? Is it that I'll die if I don't unlock the story in five minutes time? My hand shakes. The story must be more real than the cruel portraits, more palatable than a footprint in the sand, more genuine than a fossil of the unblinking eye.

46
APPLE

❧ 47 ❧

KNOWLEDGE

What I know I know by thinking my way through walls. If the colors combine to make black, so too do they diverge yet blend, holding hands as a rainbow. When a crook takes the city, there will be much lack of virtue. The truth will hide under rocks, or run about in a black cloak that won't come off. People will rush by, not seeing the hidden blessing. You and the girl in the distance are the only ones who will make it through.

48
COLLARS

"Doctor Zogotoom?"

"Yes," I said.

"Please come in. The samples are here."

I, Leopold, Zogotoom incognito, stepped into the office. It was purple as expected.

"I believe I've come to the right place," I said.

Ms. Croon nodded. "My name is Stacy Emile Croon. We've been expecting you. The young woman who works here wanted to be here when you arrived, but her cat turned pink this morning."

"I'm so sorry. She will be compensated," I said.

"That is good. Please make yourself comfortable. As you know, women do the calculations. Why did you wear pink?"

I thought about it. I winked.

Stacy nodded. "A wink will do," she said.

We sat down.

Stacy kept her eyes on me. "Not everyone is pink. In fact, you are the only pink person."

I sighed.

Stacy yawned. "I'm going fishing. Bye," she said.

What a world.

49

FIRE ESCAPE

Like a kitten chasing itself down the fire escape.

❧ 50 ❧

THE WAY

. . .

the way

leaping
running
flying
gliding
swooshing
about
the
door
you needed
to find

the way in!
the way out!
to the caverns
of your mind

leave the false

what you do
a home, a door

leaping
running
flying
gliding
swooshing

living
breathing
true

51

SOULREACH

here in the old dark
my soulreach deeploves for the
lovegrace in search of

✤ 52 ✤

CAMERA

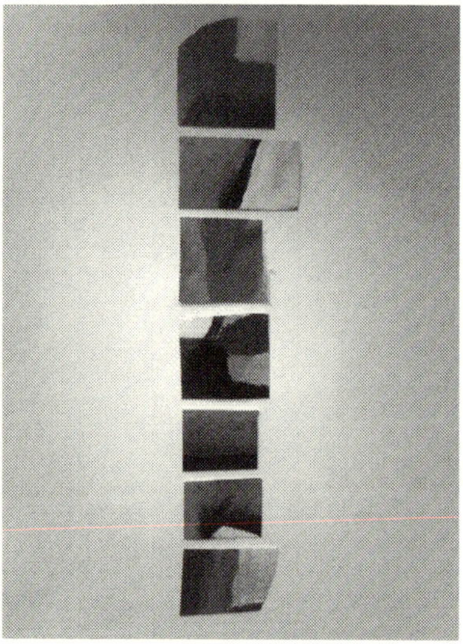

Simple enough to see when it's done.

53

54

CLOUD STORM

Wait a minute. What happened to the music? Oh, it's this way. But the door is closing. Hurry!

55
WAR

I woke as a hungry god of ancient Greece mythology, my colossal stomach digesting the many innocents I swallowed the night before. The guilt I felt for their unwitting demise filled my head like a lead blanket, poisoning my long-cultivated hopes, not to mention my intricate architectural matrices.

❦ 56 ❦

AMPLIFIED

57

THE FINE POINT

Against the marching protestors, another jab seeks to kill the struggle.

58

SOLID CHERRY?

You belong on a day when it's just stone and stillness.

59

UNDERSTOOD IN TIME

60
HUMBONGO

an array of deep swells and moon wells
carbon as the clear life
carried in a green charge
threaded through gumstick
with the little ones in their shoes

61

ZINC

62

RASPBERRY

gliding o'er a mountain face
the cagey museum of chance unexpected
it creaks and sways
like a raven clawing a berry
to become the joy of moons
glossy, long-winded
she turns without looking
like an estuary of breath
to carry the sleeper to the stars

63
WANDERER

a star falls on an underground star
to complicate the rhythm

a hand shakes like an earthquake
and

a smile flecked with dew tastes of
holy meaning while breathing the
truth-shine of the bones

64

JOURNEY

Humanity drifts through the water like seaweed.

65

HOMESPUN

Once upon a time? Once upon a time. Once and then the end.

66

RELEVANCY

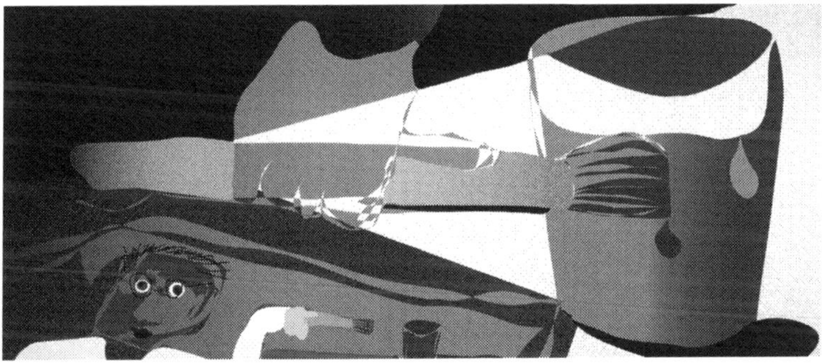

Behind the house, the sound of the truck in the dark. Workers sorting out the gas leak in the park.

67
PAINTER

I remember talking to a woman in trade school, on break between engine assembly exercises, when she was trying to learn English. In my mind-eye, I can still see those two sedans with their hoods up. Zi was from China. She asked questions about verb tenses. And I was largely clueless about

China apart from the material of a single class day that discussed: words based on pictograms, vertical text, dialect variations, the various dynasties, Confucianism, yin and yang Taoism, Buddhism, and feng shui.

68

PALE STONE

What do I write? Black turns to gray. The building houses a long hall of many doors, all closed. A woman walks towards me, wearing stilettos. She says, "I love you," as she passes, without moving her lips. I want to kiss her. The music of her voice wakes my mind and triggers the color red. And green and black. Gray is only in the outline. I turn and bolt after her. She leads the way down a steep stairwell, to a floor I've never seen. She opens the door and passes through the gap.

As she continues on, the walls turn yellow and burnt sienna. Suddenly a strange metamorphosis occurs, as I become first a frog and then a prince. My heavy jewel-laden crown I set on the floor and forget. I pursue Gloria. Nothing else matters. She looks back at me and smiles. She beckons me to come close. Her kiss to my lips lingers.

She says, "It is well."

"I love you," I say.

"It is just what I mean."

"Very noir," I say, "especially the clipped dialogue, stilettos, and sparseness of the bouquet of life."

"Then you have come to the right place, and I am the quartz. Let's have dinner at a restaurant. If time permits before the end of the ended world, I'll give you a prism. Because questions dominate, yes?"

"You mean every word and sight?"

She nodded? I couldn't tell? We ran to a restaurant? I can't remember if we ran? We had dinner? I kissed her face? She kissed my mouth? We were married within a week? I did the cooking? We changed jobs? She was elected governor? I wrote stories? Things I can't remember happened? It was good? The questions stopped?

"Hi," she said, after an absence between us, when she had gone to Portugal on business.

69

ANIMATION

70
DICTATOR

o foul dictator
why do i get the
feeling, other races
you don't want,
only yours—genocidal blood!
food for the devil!

71

72
CANCER

Why pretend?
The strings fray and break
Strength Is a Hole in the Ground
Rare as a Bean—The Lies Amass

And into the Glyphs of
a Gram or a Graph,
runs, sums, and breezes
absorb the shivers

X

a
poem like
a walk in
the park after dark?
a line drawn in sand
a terrible plan, a cough, or
a thought, or demand? i don't know.
there is no idea. one waits
like a juniper in the
grass, watching over the
stones of dreams
and fallen
stars

74

A NATURAL PRISM

75

LIBRARY

76

ROWS UPON ROWS

77

AT THE START

The past is already the future.

78

FUGACIOUS

o fugacious sky
cradle of aquiline beasts
like sweet boutonniere!

79

Keep it real.

the hero
stardust
like an eyebrow
describing
the
highest
peak

80

STEAM: THE COMMON GOOD

I disappear in your shadow.

81

HAIR

2

025. Zucchini poetry.

a bird strides quickly
about the sidewalk, like a
harried businessman.
(see?)
(and furthermore . . .)
the
sun shines
brightest on the
tree that stands the
farthest from the shadow of
the wheelbarrow that someone forgot to
seize: the red of it a fierce
reminder that nothing one assumes must
necessarily be real, so long
as the eye of
transcendental bliss borders
the gosolo
moon

82
SWEAT

The present is the undying essence of spirit whose purpose is to shepherd the Light through the Darkness of the maze.

83
SPECK

The astronauts solve the riddle; a certain man is mistaken for another until his dying day; a guy who keeps losing his hat learns a little girl found it on the subway; and life is perilous, but Gloria and I kiss and know the victory of love.

Goodbye. Good luck. Let's get together again soon.

*

AFTERWORD

I confess I'm only writing this Afterword that I might have the two extra pages I need to extend the length of the book, so I don't have to adjust the book cover dimensions. Nonetheless, I feel I have something moot enough to say that I mayn't be wasting your time. As it happens, I'm so used to writing in the voice of fiction that a paragraph or two of the unimagined is considerably novel to my way of thinking. Most fiction books are not novellas. And most novels don't have Afterwords. But my proclivity is to work the jugular and march to the beat of my own drum. What I want to say in this supplemental section is that the first edition of this book contained a considerable amount of experimental prose. However, when I had the proofs and read the story for the hundredth time, I found that part of the book far from rewarding, even though I had been happy enough in the writing of it. As a result, I determined the manuscript wasn't done after all, and after reading some Clarice Lispector, Zoran Živković, and Edgar Allan Poe to prime the pump, I transitioned into reworking the story into one I liked more. The result is the novella you have just read, and which I hope you have enjoyed as much as your favorite jovoklo kay kaderai, or otherwise imaginary treasure that you make real. Last but not least, a writer seldom gets a chance to step to the side and thank the reader for making a dream more dreamy. So if you found this story stimulating and levitational, then that is fantastic, and I step lightly off the edge of the parchment and into some other world, some other story, some other poem, in hopes of getting lucky once again.

In all robustness, blipzoing, spontaneity, fortuity, nikhedonia, enthusiasm, equilibrium, theoretics, and wonder,

Pete O'Brien

ALSO BY PETE O'BRIEN

Fiction

Arrival Day

To Dance in the Silence: A Novel[1]

The Loose Purple Tie Novellas

Myron Eberley: A Novel

Quoz: A Novelette

Sleuths in Robust Pajamas: A Novel

Squiggle

The Substantive Thief

Two Novellas

Poetry

Fields: Poems

Haiku Wonder

The Library of Oscar Strange: Poems

The Magnificent Munificence

Moon: Poems

The Old Road: Poems

Phalanx Uproar: Poems

Art

The Flavor of Art

---

1. *Sleuths in Robust Pajamas: A Novel* (first edition) was revised and published as *To Dance in the Silence: A Novel* (second edition).

ABOUT THE AUTHOR

Pete O'Brien has lived mainly in Maryland (where he currently resides), his early years in Indiana, and most of the rest in Oxford, U.K. He is a novelist, poet, and artist.

Made in the USA
Columbia, SC
11 July 2025

60636533R00114